A Celtic Psaltery

Alfred Perceval Graves

Contents

A CELTIC PSALTERY

BY

Alfred Perceval Graves

This Psaltery of Celtic Songs
To you by bounden right belongs;
For ere War's thunder round us broke,
To your content its chord I woke,
Where Cymru's Prince in fealty pure
Knelt for his Sire's Investiture.

Nor less these lays are yours but more,
In memory of the Eisteddfod floor
You flooded with a choral throng
That poured God's praise a whole day long.

But most, O Celtic Seer, to you
This Song Wreath of our Race is due,
Since high o'er hatred and division,
You have scaled the Peak and seen the Vision
Of Freedom, breaking into birth
From out an agonising Earth.

PREFACE

I have called this volume of verse a Celtic Psaltery because it mainly consists of close and free translations from Irish, Scotch Gaelic, and Welsh Poetry of a religious or serious character. The first half of the book is concerned with Irish poems. The first group of these starts with the dawning of Christianity out of Pagan darkness, and the spiritualising of the Early Irish by the wisdom to be found in the conversations between King Cormac MacArt--the Irish ancestor of our Royal Family--and his son and successor, King Carbery. Here also will be found those pregnant ninth-century utterances known as the "Irish Triads."

Next follow poems attributed or relating to some of the Irish saints--Patrick, Columba, Brigit, Moling; Lays of Monk and Hermit, Religious Invocations, Reflections and Charms and Lamentations for the Dead, including a remarkable early Irish poem entitled "The Mothers' Lament at the Slaughter of the Innocents" and a powerful peasant poem, "The Keening of Mary." The Irish section is ended by a set of songs suggested by Irish folk-tunes.

Of the early Irish Religious Poetry here translated it may be observed that the originals are not only remarkable for fine metrical form but for their cheerful spirituality, their open-air freshness and their occasional touches of kindly humour. "Irish religious poetry," it has been well said, "ranges from single quatrains to lengthy compositions dealing with all the varied aspects of religious life. Many of them give us a fascinating insight into the peculiar character of the early Irish Church, which differed in so many ways from the Christian world. We see the hermit in his lonely cell, the monk at his devotions or at his work of copying in the scriptorium or under the open sky; or we hear the ascetic who, alone or with twelve chosen companions, has left one of the great monasteries in order to live in greater solitude among the woods or mountains, or on a lonely island. The fact that so many of these poems are fathered upon well-known saints emphasises the friendly attitude of the native clergy towards vernacular poetry."[1]

I have endeavoured as far as possible to preserve in my translations both the character of these poems and their metrical form. But the latter attempt can be only a mere approximation owing to the strict rules of early Irish verse both as regards alliteration and vowel consonance. Still the use of the "inlaid rhyme" and other assonantal devices have, it is to be hoped, brought my renderings nearer in vocal effect to the originals than the use of more familiar English verse methods would have done.

The same metrical difficulties have met me when translating the Welsh sacred and spiritual poems which form the second division of this volume. But they have been more easy to grapple with--in part because I have had more assistance in dealing with the older Cymric poems from my lamented friend Mr. Sidney Richard John and other Welsh scholars, than I had in the case of the early Irish lyrics--in part because the later Welsh poems which I have rendered into English verse are generally in free, not "strict," metres, and therefore present no great difficulty to the translator.

The poems in the Welsh section are, roughly speaking, arranged in chronological order. The early Welsh poets Aneurin and Llywarch Hen are

---

1   From "The Ancient Poetry of Ireland," by Professor Kuno Meyer, to whose beautiful prose translations from Irish verse in that volume, and in his "Hail, Brigit!" I am greatly indebted.

represented by two singular pieces, Llywarch Hen's curious "Tercets" and
Aneurin's "Ode to the Months." In both of these, nature poetry and
proverbial philosophy are oddly intermingled in a manner reminiscent of
the Greek Gnomic Poets. Two examples are given of the serious verse of
Dafydd ab Gwilym, a contemporary of Chaucer, who though he did not, like
Wordsworth, read nature into human life with that spiritual insight for
which he was so remarkable, yet as a poet of fancy, the vivid, delicate,
sympathetic fancy of the Celt, still remains unmatched. Amongst
Dafydd's contemporaries and successors, Iolo Goch's noble poem, "The
Labourer," very appropriate to our breadless days, Lewis Glyn Cothi's
touching elegy on his little son John, and Dr. Sion Cent's epigrammatic
"The Noble's Grave" have been treated as far as possible in the metres
of the originals, and I have gone as near as I could to the measures of
Huw Morus' "The Bard's Death-Bed Confession," Elis Win's "Counsel in
view of Death," and the Vicar Pritchard's "A Good Wife."

A word or two about these famous Welsh writers: Huw Morus (Hugh Morris)
was the leading Welsh poet of the seventeenth century and a staunch
Royalist, who during the Civil War proved himself the equal if not the
superior of Samuel Butler as a writer of anti-Republican satire. He was
also an amatory lyrist, but closed his career as the writer of some fine
religious verses, notably this "Death-Bed Confession." Elis Win (Ellis
Wynne) was not only an excellent writer of verse but one of the masters
of Welsh prose. His "Vision of the Sleeping Bard" is, indeed, one of the
most beautifully written works in the Welsh language. Though in many
respects indebted to "Quevedo's Visions," the matter of Elis Win's book
is distinctly original, and most poetically expressed, though he is none
the less able to expose and scourge the immoralities of his age.

The Vicar Pritchard, otherwise the Rev. Rhys Pritchard, was the author
of the famous "Welshmen's Candle," "Cannwyll y Cymry," written in the
free metres, first published in 1646--completed in 1672. This consisted
of a series of moral verses in the metres of the old folk-songs

(Penillion Telyn) and remained dear to the hearts of the Welsh people for two centuries. Next may be mentioned Goronwy Owen, educated by the poet Lewis Morris, grandfather of the author of "Songs of Two Worlds" and "The Epic of Hades." As the Rev. Elvet Lewis writes of him: "Here at once we meet the true artist lost in his art. His humour is as playful as if the hand of a stern fate had never struck him on the face. His muse can laugh and make others laugh, or it can weep and make others weep." A specimen is given of one of his best known poems, "An Ode on the Day of Judgment," reproducing, as far as my powers have permitted, its final and internal rhymes and other metrical effects.

We now reach the most individual of the modern Welsh religious and philosophical poets, Islwyn (William Thomas), who took his Bardic title from the hill of Islwyn in his native Monmouthshire. He was greatly influenced by the poetry of Wordsworth, but was in no sense an imitator. Yet whilst, in the words of one of the Triads, he possessed the three things essential to poetic genius, "an eye to see nature, a heart to feel nature: and courage that dares follow nature"--he steadfastly refused to regard poetry as an art and, by declining to use the pruning-knife, allowed the finest fruits of his poetic talents to lie buried beneath immense accumulations of weedy and inferior growth. Yet what his powers were may not be ill judged of, even in translation, by the passage from his blank verse poem, "The Storm," entitled "Behind the Veil," to be found on p. 94.

Pantycelyn (the Rev. William Williams) was a co-worker with Howel Harris and Daniel Rowlands in the Methodist revival. Professor W.J. Gruffyd writes of him: "It is not enough to say he was a hymnologist--he was much more. He is the National Poet of Wales. He had certainly the loftiest imagination of all the poets of five centuries, and his influence on the Welsh people can be gauged by the fact that a good deal of his idiom or dialect has fixed itself indelibly in modern literary Welsh." The Hymn, "Marchog Jesu!" which represents him was translated by me at the request of the Committee responsible for the Institution Ceremony of the Prince of Wales at Carnarvon Castle.

Of the more modern Welsh poets represented in this volume let it be said that Ceiriog (John Hughes), so called from his birth in the Ceiriog Valley, is the Burns of Welsh Poetry. Against the spirit of gloom that the Welsh Revival cast over the first half of the nineteenth century he threw himself in sharp revolt. But while the joy of life wells up and overflows in his song he was also, like all Welshmen, serious-minded, as the specimens given in my translation from his works go to prove.

According to Professor Lewis Jones, no poem in the strict metre is more read than Eben Farrd's "Dinistur Jerusalem" ("The Destruction of Jerusalem"), translated into kindred verse in this volume, unless indeed its popularity is rivalled by Hiraethog's ode on "Heddwch," ("Peace"). Two extracts from the former poem are dealt with, and Hiraethog is represented by a beautiful fancy, "Love Divine," taken from his "Emanuel."

Finally, three living poets are represented in the Welsh section--Elvet Lewis by his stirring and touching "High Tide"; Eifion Wyn, upon whom the mantle of Ceiriog has fallen, by two exquisitely simple and pathetic poems, "Ora pro Nobis" and "A Flower-Sunday Lullaby"; and William John Gruffydd, the bright hope of "Y Beirdd Newydd" ("The New Poets"), by his poignant ballad of "The Old Bachelor of Ty'n y Mynydd."

There is no need for me to dwell upon the rest of the verse in this volume beyond stating that "The Prodigal's Return" is a free translation from a poem on that theme by an anonymous Scotch Gaelic Bard to be found in Sinton's "The Poetry of Badenoch"; that "Let there be joy!" is rendered from a Gaelic poem in Alexander Carmichael's "Carmina Gadelica," and that, finally, "Wild Wine of Nature" is a pretty close English version of a poem hardly to have been expected from that far from teetotal Scotch Gaelic Bard, Duncan Ban McIntyre.

ALFRED PERCEVAL GRAVES

RED BRANCH HOUSE
LAURISTON ROAD, WIMBLEDON
July 11, 1917

I. IRISH POEMS

THE ISLE OF THE HAPPY

(From the Early Irish)

Once when Bran, son of Feval, was with his warriors in his royal fort, they suddenly saw a woman in strange raiment upon the floor of the house. No one knew whence she had come or how she had entered, for the ramparts were closed. Then she sang these quatrains of Erin, the Isle of the Happy, to Bran while all the host were listening:

A branch I bear from Evin's apple-trees
  Whose shape agrees with Evin's orchard spray;
Yet never could her branches best belauded
  Such crystal-gauded bud and bloom display.

There is a distant Isle, deep sunk in shadows,
  Sea-horses round its meadows flash and flee;
Full fair the course, white-swelling waves enfold it,
  Four pedestals uphold it o'er the sea.

White the bronze pillars that this Fairy Curragh,[2]
  The Centuries thorough, glimmering uphold.
Through all the World the fairest land of any
  Is this whereon the many blooms unfold.

And in its midst an Ancient Tree forth flowers,
  Whence to the Hours beauteous birds outchime;
In harmony of song, with fluttering feather,
  They hail together each new birth of Time.

And through the Isle glow all glad shades of colour,
  No hue of dolour mars its beauty lone.
'Tis Silver Cloud Land that we ever name it,
  And joy and music claim it for their own.

Not here are cruel guile or loud resentment,
  But calm contentment, fresh and fruitful cheer;
Not here loud force or dissonance distressful,
  But music melting blissful on the ear.

No grief, no gloom, no death, no mortal sickness,
  Nor any weakness our sure strength can bound;
These are the signs that grace the race of Evin.
  Beneath what other heaven are they found?

A Hero fair, from out the dawn's bright blooming,
  Rides forth, illuming level shore and flood;
The white and seaward plain he sets in motion,
  He stirs the ocean into burning blood.

A host across the clear blue sea comes rowing,
  Their prowess showing, till they touch the shore;

---

2   Plain or tableland such as the Curragh of Kildare.

Thence seek the Shining Stone where Music's measure
  Prolongs the pleasure of the pulsing oar.

It sings a strain to all the host assembled;
  That strain untired has trembled through all time!
It swells with such sweet choruses unnumbered,
  Decay and Death have slumbered since its chime.

Thus happiness with wealth is o'er us stealing,
  And laughter pealing forth from every hill.
Yea! through the Land of Peace at every season
  Pure Joy and Reason are companions still.

Through all the lovely Isle's unchanging hours
  There showers and showers a stream of silver bright;
A pure white cliff that from the breast of Evin
  Mounts up to Heaven thus assures her light.

Long ages hence a Wondrous Child and Holy,
  Yet in estate most lowly shall have birth;
Seed of a Woman, yet whose Mate knows no man
  To rule the thousand thousands of the earth.

His sway is ceaseless; 'twas His love all-seeing
  That Earth's vast being wrought with perfect skill.
All worlds are His; for all His kindness cares;
  But woe to all gainsayers of His Will.

The stainless heavens beneath His Hands unfolded,
  He moulded Man as free of mortal stain,
And even now Earth's sin-struck sons and daughters
  His Living Waters can make whole again.

Not unto all of you is this my message
  Of marvellous presage at this hour revealed.
Let Bran but listen from Earth's concourse crowded
  Unto the shrouded wisdom there concealed.

Upon a couch of languor lie not sunken,
  Beware lest drunkenness becloud thy speech!
Put forth, O Bran, across the far, clear waters.
  And Evin's daughters haply thou may'st reach.

THE WISDOM OF KING CORMAC

(From the Early Irish)

THE DEPTHS OF KING CORMAC'S HEART

CARBERY

"Cormac, Conn's grandson, and son of great Art
Declare to me now from the depths of thy heart,
  With the wise and the foolish,
    With strangers and friends,
  The meek and the mulish,
    The old and the young,
  With good manners to make God amends--
    How I must govern my tongue,
  And in all things comport myself purely,
    The good and the wicked among."

CORMAC

"The answer thereto is not difficult surely.
Be not too wise nor too scatter-brained,
Not too conceited nor too restrained,
Be not too haughty nor yet too meek,
Too tattle-tongued or too loth to speak,
Neither too hard nor yet too weak.
If too wise you appear, folk too much will claim of you,
If too foolish, they still will be making fresh game of you,
If too conceited, vexatious they'll dub you,
If too unselfish, they only will snub you,
If too much of a tattler, you ne'er will be heeded,
If too silent, your company ne'er will be needed,
If overhard, your pride will be broken asunder,
If overweak, the folk will trample you under."

THE HOUSE OF HOSPITALITY

CARBERY

"Cormac, grandson of Conn, what dues hath a
    Chief and an ale-house?"
Said Cormac: "Not hard to tell!
Good behaviour around a good Chief;
Lamps to light for the eye's relief;
Exerting ourselves for the Company's sake,
Seats assigned with no clownish mistake,
Deft and liberal measuring carvers;
Attentive and nimble-handed servers;

Moderation in music and song;
A telling of stories not too long;
The Host, to a bright elation stirred,
Giving each guest a welcoming word.
Silence during the Bard's reciting--
Each chorus in sweet concent uniting."

HOW KING CORMAC ORDERED HIS YOUTH

CARBERY

"O Cormac, grandson of Conn, say sooth,
How didst thou order thy days in youth?"

CORMAC

"Into the woods I went a-listening,
I was a gazer when stars were glistening;
Blind when secrets were plain to guess;
A silent one in the wilderness;
I was talkative with the many,
Yet, in the mead-hall, milder than any;
I was stern amid battle cries;
I was gentle towards allies;
I was a doctor unto the sick;
On the feeble I laid no stick.
Not close lest burdensome I should be;
Though wise not given to arrogancy.
I promised little, though lavish of gift;
I was not reckless though I was swift;

Young, I never derided the old;
And never boasted though I was bold;
Of an absent one no ill would I tell;
I would not reproach, though I praised full well;
I never would ask but ever would give,
For a kingly life I craved to live!"

THE WORST WAY OF PLEADING

CARBERY

"O Cormac Mac Art, of Wisdom exceeding,
What is the evilest way of pleading?"
Said Cormac: "Not hard to tell!
Against knowledge contending;
Without proofs, pretending;
In bad language escaping;
A style stiff and scraping;
Speech mean and muttering,
Hair-splitting and stuttering;
Uncertain proofs devising;
Authorities despising;
Scorning custom's reading;
Confusing all your pleading;
To madness a mob to be leading;
With the shout of a strumpet
Blowing one's own trumpet."

KING CORMAC'S WORST ENEMY

"O Cormac Mac Art, of your enemies' garrison,
Who is the worst for your witty comparison?"
  Said Cormac: "Not hard to tell!
A man with a satirist's nameless audacity;
A man with a slave-woman's shameless pugnacity;
One with a dirty dog's careless up-bound,
The conscience thereto of a ravening hound.
Like a stately noble he answers all speakers
From a memory full as a Chronicle-maker's,
With the suave behaviour of Abbot or Prior,
Yet the blasphemous tongue of a horse-thief liar
And he wise as false in every grey hair,
Violent, garrulous, devil-may-care.
When he cries, 'The case is settled and over!'
Though you were a saint, I swear you would swear!"

IRISH TRIADS

(By an unknown Author of the ninth century)

Three signs whereby to mark a man of vice
Are hatred, bitterness, and avarice.

Three graceless sisters in the bond of unity
Are lightness, flightiness, and importunity.

Three clouds, the most obscuring Wisdom's glance,
Forgetfulness, half-knowledge, ignorance.

Three savage sisters sharpening life's distress,
Foul Blasphemy, Foul Strife, Foul-mouthedness.

Three services the worst for human hands,
A vile Lord's, a vile Lady's, a vile Land's.

Three gladnesses that soon give way to griefs,
A wooer's, a tale-bearer's, and a thief's.

Three signs of ill-bred folk in every nation--
A visit lengthened to a visitation,
Staring, and overmuch interrogation.

Three arts that constitute a true physician:
To cure your malady with expedition.
To let no after-consequence remain,
And make his diagnosis without pain.

Three keys that most unlock our secret thinking
Are love and trustfulness and overdrinking.

Three nurses of hot blood to man's undoing--
Excess of pride, of drinking, and of wooing.

Three the receivers are of stolen goods:
A cloak, the cloak of night, the cloak of woods.

Three unions, each of peace a proved miscarriage,
Confederate feats, joint ploughland, bonds of marriage.

Three lawful hand-breadths for mankind about the body be,
From shoes to hose, from ear to hair, from tunic unto knee.

Three youthful sisters for all eyes to see,
Beauty, desire, and generosity.

Three excellences of our dress are these--
Elegance, durability, and ease.

Three idiots of a bad guest-house are these--
A hobbling beldam with a hoicking wheeze,
A brainless tartar of a serving-girl,
For serving-boy a swinish lubber-churl.

Three slender ones whereon the whole earth swings--
The thin milk stream that in the keeler sings;
The thin green blade that from the cornfield springs;
That thin grey thread the housewife's shuttle flings.

The three worst welcomes that will turn a guest-house
For weary wayfarers into a Pest-house--
Within its roof a workman's hammer beat;
A bath of scalding water for your feet;
With no assuaging draught, salt food to eat.

Three finenesses that foulness keep from sight--
Fine manners in the most misfeatured wight;
Fine shapes of art by servile fingers moulded;
Fine wisdom from a cripple's brain unfolded.

Three fewnesses that better are than plenty:
A fewness of fine words--but one in twenty;
A fewness of milch cows, when grass is shrinking;

Fewness of friends when beer is best for drinking.

Three worst of snares upon a Chieftain's way:
Sloth, treachery, and evil counsel they!

Three ruins of a tribe to west or east:
A lying Chief, false Brehon, lustful Priest.

The rudest three of all the sons of earth:
A youngster of an old man making mirth;
A strong man at a sick man poking fun;
A wise man gibing at a foolish one.

Three signs that show a fop: the comb-track on his hair;
The track of his nice teeth upon his nibbled fare;
His cane-track on the dust, oft as he takes the air.

Three sparks that light the fire of love are these--
Glamour of face, and grace, and speech of ease.

Three steadinesses of wise womanhood--
steady tongue through evil, as through good;
A steady chastity, whoso else shall stray;
Steady house service, all and every day.

Three sounds of increase: kine that low,
When milk unto their calves they owe;
The hammer on the anvil's brow,
The pleasant swishing of the plough.

Three sisters false: I would! I might! I may!
Three fearful brothers: Hearken! Hush! and Stay!

Three coffers of a depth unknown
Are his who occupies the throne,
The Church's, and the privileged Poet's own.

Three glories of a gathering free from strife--
Swift hound, proud steed, and beautiful young wife.

The world's three laughing-stocks (be warned and wiser!)--
An angry man, a jealoused, and a miser.

Three powers advantaging a Chieftain most
Are Peace and Justice and an Armed Host.

Lays of the Irish Saints

ST. PATRICK'S BLESSING ON MUNSTER

(From the Early Irish)

Blessing from the Lord on High
Over Munster fall and lie;
To her sons and daughters all
Choicest blessing still befall;
Fruitful blessing on the soil
That supports her faithful toil.

Blessing full of ruddy health,
Blessing full of every wealth
That her borders furnish forth,
East and west and south and north;
Blessing from the Lord on High
Over Munster fall and lie!

Blessing on her peaks in air,
Blessing on her flagstones bare,
Blessing from her ridges flow
To her grassy glens below!
Blessing from the Lord on High
Over Munster fall and lie!

As the sands upon her shore
Underneath her ships, for store,
Be her hearths, a twinkling host,
Over mountain, plain and coast;
Blessings from the Lord on High
Over Munster fall and lie!

THE BREASTPLATE OF ST. PATRICK

Otherwise called "The Deer's Cry." For St. Patrick sang this hymn when
the ambuscades were laid against him by King Leary that he might go to
Tara to sow the Faith. Then it seemed to those lying in ambush that he
and his monks were wild deer with a fawn, even Benen (Benignus)
following him.

I invoke, upon my path
To the King of Ireland's rath,
  The Almighty Power of the Trinity;
Through belief in the Threeness,
Through confession of the Oneness
  Of the Maker's Eternal Divinity.

I invoke, on my journey arising,
The power of Christ's Birth and Baptizing,
The powers of the hours of His dread Crucifixion,
  Of His Death and Abode in the Tomb,
The power of the hour of His glorious Resurrection
  From out the Gehenna of gloom,
The power of the hour when to Heaven He ascended,
And the power of the hour when by Angels attended,
  He returns for the Judgment of Doom!
    On my perilous way
    To Tara to-day,
    I, Patrick, God's servant,
      Invoke from above
      The Cherubim's love!
Yea! I summon the might of the Company fervent
Of Angel obedient, ministrant Archangel
To speed and to prosper my Irish Evangel.
I go forth on my path in the trust
Of the gathering to God of the Just;
In the power of the Patriarchs' prayers;
The foreknowledge of Prophets and Seers;
The Apostles' pure preaching;
The Confessors' sure teaching;
The virginity blest of God's Dedicate Daughters,
And the lives and the deaths of His Saints and His Martyrs!

I arise to-day in the strength of the heaven,
  The glory of the sun,
  The radiance of the moon,
The splendour of fire and the swiftness of the levin,
The wind's flying force,
  The depth of the sea,
The earth's steadfast course,
  The rock's austerity.

I arise on my way,
With God's Strength for my stay,
God's Might to protect me,
God's Wisdom to direct me,
God's Eye to be my providence,
God's Ear to take my evidence,
God's Word my words to order,
God's Hand to be my warder,
God's Way to lie before me,
God's Shield and Buckler o'er me,
God's Host Unseen to save me,
  From each ambush of the Devil,
    From each vice that would enslave me.
And from all who wish me evil,
  Whether far I fare or near.
  Alone or in a multitude.

All these Hierarchies and Powers
  I invoke to intervene,
When the adversary lowers
  On my path, with purpose keen
  Of vengeance black and bloody
  On my soul and my body;
I bind these Powers to come

Against druid counsel dark,
The black craft of Pagandom,
  And the false heresiarch,
The spells of wicked women,
  And the wizard's arts inhuman,
  And every knowledge, old and fresh,
  Corruptive of man's soul and flesh.

May Christ, on my way
To Tara to-day,
Shield me from prison,
  Shield me from fire,
Drowning or wounding
  By enemy's ire,
So that mighty fruition
May follow my mission.
Christ behind and before me,
Christ beneath me and o'er me,
Christ within and without me,
Christ around and about me,
Christ on my left and Christ on my right,
Christ with me at morn and Christ with me at night;
Christ in each heart that shall ever take thought of me,
Christ in each mouth that shall ever speak aught of me;
Christ in each eye that shall ever on me fasten,
Christ in each ear that shall ever to me listen.

  I invoke, upon my path
  To the King of Ireland's rath,
    The Almighty Power of the Trinity;
  Through belief in the Threeness,
  Through confession of the Oneness
    Of the Maker's Eternal Divinity.

ST. PATRICK'S EVENSONG

Christ, Thou Son of God most High,
  May thy Holy Angels keep
Watch around us as we lie
  In our shining beds asleep.

Time's hid veil with truth to pierce
  Let them teach our dreaming eyes,
Arch-King of the Universe,
  High-Priest of the Mysteries.

May no demon of the air,
  May no malice of our foes,
Evil dream or haunting care
  Mar our willing, prompt repose!

May our vigils hallowed be
  By the tasks we undertake!
May our sleep be fresh and free,
  Without let and without break.

ST. COLUMBA'S GREETING TO IRELAND

(An old Irish poem recounting the Saint's voyage from Erin to Alba
(Scotland), from which he but once returned)

Delightful to stand on the brow of Ben Edar,
  Before being a speeder on the white-haired sea!
The dashing of the wave in wild disorder
  On its desolate border delightful to me!

Delightful to stand on the brow of Ben Edar,
  After being a speeder o'er the white-bosomed sea,
After rowing and rowing in my little curragh!
  To the loud shore thorough, O, Och, Ochonee!

Great is the speed of my little wherry,
  As afar from Derry its path it ploughs;
Heavy my heart out of Erin steering
  And nearing Alba of the beetling brows.

My foot is fast in my chiming curragh,
  Tears of sorrow my sad heart fill.
Who lean not on God are but feeble-minded,
  Without His Love we go blinded still.

There is a grey eye that tears are thronging,
  Fixed with longing on Erin's shore,
It shall never see o'er the waste of waters
  The sons and daughters of Erin more.

Its glance goes forth o'er the brine wave-broken,
  Far off from the firm-set, oaken seat;
Many the tears from that grey eye streaming,
  The faint, far gleaming of Erin to meet.

For indeed my soul is set upon Erin,
  And all joys therein from Linnhe to Lene,
On each pleasant prospect of proud Ultonia,
  Mild Momonia and Meath the green.

In Alba eastward the lean Scot increases,
  Frequent the diseases and murrain in her parts,
Many in her mountains the scanty-skirted fellows,
  Many are the hard and the jealous hearts.

Many in the West are our Kings and Princes noble,
  Orchards bend double beneath their fruitage vast;
Sloes upon the thorn-bush shine in blue abundance,
  Oaks in redundance drop the royal mast.

Melodious are her clerics, melodious Erin's birds are,
  Gentle her youths' words are, her seniors discreet;
Famed far her chieftains--goodlier are no men--
  Very fair her women for espousal sweet.

'Tis within the West sweet Brendan is residing,
  There Colum MacCriffan is indeed abiding now;
And 'tis unto the West ruddy Baithir is repairing
  And Adamnan shall be faring to perform his vow.

Salute them courteously, salute them all and single,
  After them Comgall, Eternity's true heir,
Then to the stately Monarch of fair Navan

Up from the haven my greeting greatly bear.

My blessing, fair youth, and my full benediction
  Without one restriction be bearing to-day--
One half above Erin, one half seven times over,
  And one half above Alba to hover for aye.

Carry to Erin that full load of blessing,
  For sorrow distressing my heart's pulses fail,
If Death overtake me, the whole truth be spoken!
  My heart it was broken by great love for the Gael.

"Gael, Gael," at that dear word's repeating,
  Again with glad beating my heart takes my breast.
Beloved is Cummin of the tresses most beauteous,
  And Cainnech the duteous and Comgall the Blest.

Were all of Alba mine now to enter,
  Mine from the centre and through to the sea;
I would rather possess in deep-leaved Derry
  The home that was very very dear to me.

To Derry my love is ever awarded,
  For her lawns smooth-swarded, her pure clear wells,
And the hosts of angels that hover and hover
  Over and over her oak-set dells.

Indeed and indeed for these joys I love her,
  Pure air is above her, smooth turf below;
While evermore over each oak-bough leafy
  A beautiful bevy of angels go.

My Derry, my little oak grove of Erin!
  My dwelling was therein, my small dear cell.
Strike him, O Living God out of Heaven,
  With Thy red Levin who works them ill.

Beloved shall Derry and Durrow endure,
  Beloved Raphoe of the pure clear well,
Beloved Drumhome with its sweet acorn showers,
  Beloved the towers of Swords and Kells!

Beloved too at my heart as any
  Art thou Drumcliffe on Culcinne's strand,
And over Loch Foyle--'tis delight to be gazing--
  So shapely are her shores on either hand.

Delightful indeed, is the purple sea's glamour,
  Where sea-gulls clamour in white-winged flight,
As you view it afar from Derry beloved,
  O the peace of it, the peace and delight!

ST. COLUMBA IN IONA

(From an Irish Manuscript in the Burgundian Library, Brussels)

Delightful would it be to me
  From a rock pinnacle to trace
Continually
  The Ocean's face:
That I might watch the heaving waves
  Of noble force
To God the Father chant their staves
  Of the earth's course.
That I might mark its level strand,
  To me no lone distress,
That I might hark the sea-bird's wondrous band--
  Sweet source of happiness.
That I might hear the clamorous billows thunder
  On the rude beach.
That by my blessed church side I might ponder
  Their mighty speech.
Or watch surf-flying gulls the dark shoal follow
  With joyous scream,
Or mighty ocean monsters spout and wallow,
  Wonder supreme!
That I might well observe of ebb and flood
  All cycles therein;
And that my mystic name might be for good
  But "Cul-ri. Erin."
That gazing toward her on my heart might fall
  A full contrition,
That I might then bewail my evils all,

Though hard the addition;
That I might bless the Lord who all things orders
  For their great good.
The countless hierarchies through Heaven's bright borders--
  Land, strand, and flood,
That I might search all books and from their chart
  Find my soul's calm;
Now kneel before the Heaven of my heart,
  Now chant a psalm;
Now meditate upon the King of Heaven,
  Chief of the Holy Three;
Now ply my work by no compulsion driven.
  What greater joy could be?
Now plucking dulse upon the rocky shore,
  Now fishing eager on,
Now furnishing food unto the famished poor;
  In hermitage anon:
The guidance of the King of Kings
  Has been vouchsafed unto me;
If I keep watch beneath His wings,
  No evil shall undo me.

HAIL, BRIGIT!

An old Irish poem on the Hill of Alenn recording the disappearance of the Pagan World of Ireland and the triumph of Christianity by the establishment at Kildare of the convent of Brigit, Saint and Princess.

  Safe on thy throne,
Triumphing Bride,
Down Liffey's side,
Far to the coast,
Rule with the host
Under thy care
Over the Children of Mighty Cathair.

  God's hid intents
At every time,
For pure Erin's clime
All telling surpass.
Liffey's clear glass
Mirrors thy reign,
But many proud masters have passed from his plain.

  When on his banks
I cast my eyes thorough
The fair, grassy Curragh,
Awe enters my mind
At each wreck that I find
Around me far strown
Of lofty kings' palaces gaunt, lichen-grown!

Laery was monarch
As far as the Main;
Vast Ailill's reign!
The Curragh's green wonder
Still grows the blue under,
The old rulers thereon
One after other to cold death have gone.

Where is Alenn far-famed,
How dear in delights!
Beneath her what Knights
What Princes repose
How feared by her foes
When Crimthan was Chief--
Crimthan of Conquests--now passes belief!

Proudly the triumph-shout
Rang from his victor lords,
Round their massed shock of swords;
While their foes' serried, blue
Spears they struck through and through;
Blasts of delight
Blared from their horns over hundreds in flight.

Blithe, on their anvils
Even-hued, blent
The hammers' concent;
From the Brugh the bard's song
Brake sweet and strong;
Proud beauty graced
The field where knights jousted and charioteers raced.

There in each household
Ran the rich mead;
Steed neighed to steed;
Chains jingled again
Unto Kings among men
Under the blades
Of their five-edged, long, bitter, blood-letting spear-heads.

There, at each hour,
Harp music o'erflowed;
The wine-galleon rode
The violet sea,
Whence silver showered free,
And gold torques without fail,
From the land of the Gaul to the Land of the Gael.

To Britain's far coasts
The renown of those kings
On a meteor's wings
O'er the waters had flown.
Yea! Alenn's high throne,
With its masterful lore,
Made sport of the pomp of each palace before.

But where, oh, where is mighty Cathair?
Before him or since
No shapelier Prince
Ruled many-hued Erin.
Though round the rath, wherein
They laid him, you cry,
The Champion of Champions can never reply.

Where is Feradach's robe,
Where his diadem famed,
Round which, as it flamed,
Plumed ranks deployed?
His blue helm is destroyed,
His shining cloak dust.
Overthrower of kings, in whom now is thy trust?

Alenn's worship of auguries
Now is as naught!
None thereof takes thought.
All in vain is each spell
The dark future to tell!
All is vain, when 'tis probed,
And Alenn lies dead of her black arts disrobed.

Hail, Brigit! whose lands
To-day I behold,
Whither monarchs of old
Came each in his turn.
Thy fame shall outburn
Their mightiest glory;
Thou art over them all, till this Earth ends its story.

Yea! Thy rule with the King
Everlasting shall stand,
Apart from the land
Of thy burial-place.
Child of Bresal's proud race,
O triumphing Bride,[3]
Sit safely enthroned upon Liffey's green side.

---

3   Brigit; hence St. Bride's Bay.

THE DEVIL'S TRIBUTE TO MOLING

(From the Early Irish)

Once, when St. Moling was praying in his church, the Devil visited him in purple raiment and distinguished form. On being challenged by the saint, he declared himself to be the Christ, but on Moling's raising the Gospel to disprove his claim, the Evil One confessed that he was Satan. "Wherefore hast thou come?" asked Moling. "For a blessing," the Devil replied. "Thou shalt not have it," said Moling, "for thou deservest it not." "Well, then," said the Devil, "bestow the full of a curse on me." "What good were that to thee?" asked Moling. "The venom and the hurt of the curse will be on the lips from which it will come." After further parley, the Devil paid this tribute to Moling:

He is pure gold, the sky around the sun,
  A silver chalice brimmed with blessed wine,
  An Angel shape, a book of lore divine,
Whoso obeys in all the Eternal One.

He is a foolish bird that fowlers lime,
  A leaking ship in utmost jeopardy,
  An empty vessel and a withered tree,
Who disobeys the Sovereign Sublime.

A fragrant branch with blossoms overrun,
  A bounteous bowl with honey overflowing,
  A precious stone, of virtue past all knowing
Is he who doth the will of God's dear Son.

A nut that only emptiness doth fill,
  A sink of foulness, a crookt branch is he
  Upon a blossomless crab-apple tree,
Who doeth not his Heavenly Master's will.

Whoso obeys the Son of God and Mary--
  He is a sunflash lighting up the moor,
  He is a dais on the Heavenly Floor,
A pure and very precious reliquary.

A sun heaven-cheering he, in whose warm beam
  The King of Kings takes ever fresh delight,
  He is a temple, noble, blessed, bright,
A saintly shrine with gems and gold a-gleam.

The altar he, whence bread and wine are told,
  While countless melodies around are hymned,
  A chalice cleansed from God's own grapes upbrimmed,
Upon Christ's garment's hem the joyful gold.

THE HYMN OF ST. PHILIP

(From the Early Irish)

Philip the Apostle holy
  At an Aonach[4] once was telling
Of the immortal birds and shapely
  Afar in Inis Eidheand dwelling.

East of Africa abiding
  They perform a labour pleasant;
Unto earth there comes no colour
  That on their pinions is not present.

Since the fourth Creation morning
  When their God from dust outdrew them,
Not one plume has from them perished,
  And not one bird been added to them.

Seven fair streams with all their channels
  Pierce the plains wherethrough they flutter,
Round whose banks the birds go feeding,
  Then soar thanksgiving songs to utter.

Midnight is their hour apportioned,
  When, on magic coursers mounted,
Through the starry skies they circle,
  To chants of angel choirs uncounted.

Of the foremost birds the burthen

---

4   A fair, or open-air assembly.

Most melodiously unfolded
Tells of all the works of wonder
  God wrought before the world He moulded.

Then a sweet crowd heavenward lifted,
  When the nocturn bells are pealing,
Chants His purposes predestined
  Until the Day of Doom's revealing.

Next a flock whose thoughts are blessed,
  Under twilight's curls dim sweeping,
Hymn God's wondrous words of Judgment
  When His Court of Doom is keeping.

One and forty on a hundred
  And a thousand, without lying,
Was their number, joined to virtue,
  Put upon each bird-flock flying.

Who these faultless birds should hearken,
  Thus their strains of rapture linking,
For the very transport of it,
  Unto death would straight be sinking.

Pray for us, O mighty Mary!
  When earth's bonds no more are binding,
That these birds our souls may solace,
  In the Land of Philip's finding.

THE SCRIBE

(From the Early Irish)

For weariness my hand writes ill,
  My small sharp quill runs rough and slow;
Its slender beak with failing craft
  Gives forth its draught of dark blue flow.

And yet God's blessed wisdom gleams
  And streams beneath my fair brown palm,
The while quick jets of holly ink
  The letters link of prayer or psalm.

So still my dripping pen is fain
  To cross the plain of parchment white,
Unceasing, at some rich man's call,
  Till wearied all am I to-night.

THE HERMIT'S SONG

(See *Eriu*, vol. I, p. 39, where the Irish text will be found. It dates
from the ninth century)

I long, O Son of the living God,
  Ancient, eternal King,
For a hidden hut on the wilds untrod,
  Where Thy praises I might sing;
A little, lithe lark of plumage grey
  To be singing still beside it,
Pure waters to wash my sin away,
  When Thy Spirit has sanctified it.
Hard by it a beautiful, whispering wood
  Should stretch, upon either hand,
To nurse the many-voiced fluttering brood
  In its shelter green and bland.
Southward, for warmth, should my hermitage face,
  With a runnel across its floor,
In a choice land gifted with every grace,
  And good for all manner of store.
A few true comrades I next would seek
  To mingle with me in prayer,
Men of wisdom, submissive, meek;
  Their number I now declare,
Four times three and three times four,
  For every want expedient,
Sixes two within God's Church door,
  To north and south obedient;
Twelve to mingle their voices with mine
  At prayer, whate'er the weather,

To Him Who bids His dear sun shine
  On the good and ill together.
Pleasant the Church with fair Mass cloth,
  No dwelling for Christ's declining
To its crystal candles, of bees-wax both,
  On the pure, white Scriptures shining.
Beside it a hostel for all to frequent,
  Warm with a welcome for each,
Where mouths, free of boasting and ribaldry, vent
  But modest and innocent speech.
These aids to support us my husbandry seeks,
  I name them now without hiding--
Salmon and trout and hens and leeks,
  And the honey-bees' sweet providing.
Raiment and food enow will be mine
  From the King of all gifts and all graces;
And I to be kneeling, in rain or shine,
  Praying to God in all places.

CRINOG

A.D. 900-1000

This poem relates "to one who lived like a sister or spiritual wife with
a priest, monk, or hermit, a practice which, while early suppressed and
abandoned everywhere else, seems to have survived in the Irish Church
till the tenth century."

Crinog of melodious song,
  No longer young, but bashful-eyed,
As when we roved Niall's Northern Land,
  Hand in hand, or side by side.

Peerless maid, whose looks ran o'er
  With the lovely lore of Heaven,
By whom I slept in dreamless joy,
  A gentle boy of summers seven.

We dwelt in Banva's broad domain,
  Without one stain of soul or sense;
While still mine eye flashed forth on thee
  Affection free of all offence.

To meet thy counsel quick and just,
  Our faithful trust responsive springs;
Better thy wisdom's searching force
  Than any smooth discourse with kings.

In sinless sisterhood with men,
  Four times since then, hast thou been bound,

Yet not one rumour of ill-fame
  Against thy name has travelled round.

At last, their weary wanderings o'er,
  To me once more thy footsteps tend;
The gloom of age makes dark thy face,
  Thy life of grace draws near its end.

O, faultless one and very dear,
  Unstinted welcome here is thine.
Hell's haunting dread I ne'er shall feel,
  So thou be kneeling at my side.

Thy blessed fame shall ever bide,
  For far and wide thy feet have trod.
Could we their saintly track pursue,
  We yet should view the Living God.

You leave a pattern and bequest
  To all who rest upon the earth--
A life-long lesson to declare
  Of earnest prayer the precious worth.

God grant us peace and joyful love!
  And may the countenance of Heaven's King
Beam on us when we leave behind
  Our bodies blind and withering.

KING AND HERMIT

Marvan, brother of King Guare of Connaught, in the seventh century, had renounced the life of a warrior prince for that of a hermit. The King endeavoured to persuade his brother to return to his Court, when the following colloquy took place between them:

GUARE

Now Marvan, hermit of the grot,
  Why sleep'st thou not on quilted feathers?
Why on a pitch-pine floor instead
  At night make head against all weathers?

MARVAN

I have a shieling in the wood,
  None save my God has knowledge of it,
An ash-tree and a hazelnut
  Its two sides shut, great oak-boughs roof it.

Two heath-clad posts beneath a buckle
  Of honeysuckle its frame are propping,
The woods around its narrow bound
  Swine-fattening mast are richly dropping.

From out my shieling not too small,
  Familiar all, fair paths invite me;
Now, blackbird, from my gable end,
  Sweet sable friend, thy notes delight me.

With joys the stags of Oakridge leap
  Into their clear and deep-banked river,
Far off red Roiny glows with joy,
  Muckraw, Moinmoy in sunshine quiver.

With mighty mane a green-barked yew
  Upholds the blue; his fortress green
An oak uprears against the storms,
  Tremendous forms, stupendous scene.

Mine apple-tree is full of fruit
  From crown to root--a hostel's store--
My bonny nutful hazel-bush
  Leans branching lush against my door.

A choice, pure spring of cooling draught
  Is mine. What prince has quaffed a rarer?
Around it cresses keen, O King,
  Invite the famishing wayfarer.

Tame swine and wild and goat and deer
  Assemble here upon its brink,
Yea! even the badger's brood draw near
  And without fear lie down to drink.

A peaceful troop of creatures strange,
  They hither range from wood and height,
To meet them slender foxes steal
  At vesper peal, O my delight!

These visitants as to a Court
  Frequent resort to seek me out,
Pure water, Brother Guare, are they

The salmon grey, the speckled trout;

Red rowans, dusky sloes and mast--
  O unsurpassed and God-sent dish--
Blackberries, whortleberries blue,
  Red strawberries to my taste and wish;

Sweet apples, honey of wild bees
  And after them of eggs a clutch,
Haws, berries of the juniper;
  Who, King, could cast a slur on such?

A cup with mead of hazelnut
  Outside my hut in summer shine,
Or ale with herbs from wood and spring
  Are worth, O King, thy costliest wine.

Bright bluebells o'er my board I throw--
  A lovely show my feast to spangle--
The rushes' radiance, oaklets grey,
  Brier-tresses gay, sweet, goodly tangle.

When brilliant summer casts once more
  Her cloak of colour o'er the fields,
Sweet-tasting marjoram, pignut, leek,
  To all who seek, her verdure yields.

Her bright red-breasted little men
  Their lovely music then outpour,
The thrush exults, the cuckoos all
  Around her call and call once more.

The bees, earth's small musicians, hum,
  No longer dumb, in gentle chorus.
Like echoes faint of that long plaint
  The fleeing wild-fowl murmur o'er us.

The wren, an active songster now,
  From off the hazel-bough pipes shrill,
Woodpeckers flock in multitudes
  With beauteous hoods and beating bill.

With fair white birds, the crane and gull
  The fields are full, while cuckoos cry--
No mournful music! Heath-poults dun
  Through russet heather sunward fly.

The heifers now with loud delight,
  Summer bright, salute thy reign!
Smooth delight for toilsome loss
  'Tis now to cross the fertile plain.

The warblings of the wind that sweep
  From branchy wood to beaming sky,
The river-falls, the swan's far note--
  Delicious music floating by.

Earth's bravest band because unhired,
  All day, untired make cheer for me.
In Christ's own eyes of endless youth
  Can this same truth be said of thee?

What though in Kingly pleasures now
  Beyond all riches thou rejoice,
Content am I my Saviour good

Should on this wood have set my choice.

Without one hour of war or strife
  Through all my life at peace I fare;
Where better can I keep my tryst
  With our Lord Christ, O brother Guare?

GUARE

My glorious Kingship, yea! and all
  My Sire's estates that fall to me,
My Marvan, I would gladly give,
  So I might live my life with thee.

ON AENGUS THE CULDEE

Author of the **Felire AEngusa** or Calendar of Church Festivals. He was a
Saint, his appellation Culdee [Ceile de] meaning "Servant of God." He
lived at the end of the eighth and beginning of the ninth century.

Delightful here at Disert Bethel,
  By cold, pure Nore at peace to rest,
Where noisy raids have never sullied
  The beechen forest's virgin vest.

For here the Angel Host would visit
  Of yore with AEngus, Oivlen's son,

As in his cross-ringed cell he lauded
  The One in Three, the Three in One.

To death he passed upon a Friday,
  The day they slew our Blessed Lord.
Here stands his tomb; unto the Assembly
  Of Holy Heaven his soul has soared.

'Twas in Cloneagh he had his rearing;
  'Tis in Cloneagh he now lies dead,
'Twas in Cloneagh of many crosses
  That first his psalms he read.

THE SHAVING OF MURDOCH

(From the Early Irish)

(By Muiredach O'Daly, late twelfth century, when he and Cathal More of the Red Hand, King of Connaught, entered the monastic life together.)

Murdoch, whet thy razor's edge,
  Our crowns to pledge to Heaven's Ardrigh!
Vow we now our hair fine-tressed
  To the Blessed Trinity!

Now my head I shear to Mary;
  'Tis a true heart's very due.
Shapely, soft-eyed Chieftain now

Shear thy brow to Mary, too!

Seldom on thy head, fair Chief,
  Hath a barbing-knife been plied;
Oft the fairest of Princesses
  Combed her tresses at thy side.

Whensoever we did bathe,
  We found no scathe, yourself and I,
With Brian of the well-curled locks,
  From hidden rocks and currents wry.

And most I mind what once befell
  Beside the well of fair Boru--
I swam a race with Ua Chais
  The icy flood of Fergus through.

When hand to hand the bank we reached,
  Swift foot to foot we stretched again,
Till Duncan Cairbre, Chief of Chiefs,
  Gave us three knives--not now in vain.

No other blades such temper have;
  Then, Murdoch, shave with easy art!
Whet, Cathal of the Wine Red Hand,
  Thy Victor brand, in peaceful part!

Then our shorn heads from weather wild
  Shield, Daughter mild of Joachim!
Preserve us from the sun's fierce power,
  Mary, soft Flower of Jesse's Stem!

ON THE FLIGHTINESS OF THOUGHT

(A tenth-century poem. See *Eriu*, vol. iii, p. 13)

Shame upon my thoughts, O shame!
  How they fly in order broken,
Therefore much I fear for blame
  When the Trump of Doom has spoken.

At my psalms, they oft are set
  On a path the Fiend must pave them;
Evermore, with fash and fret,
  In God's sight they misbehave them.

Through contending crowds they fleet,
  Companies of wanton women,
Silent wood or strident street,
  Swifter than the breezes skimming.

Now through paths of loveliness,
  Now through ranks of shameful riot,
Onward evermore they press,
  Fledged with folly and disquiet.

O'er the Ocean's sounding deep
  Now they flash like fiery levin;
Now at one vast bound they leap
  Up from earth into the Heaven.

Thus afar and near they roam
  On their race of idle folly;

Till at last to reason's home
  They return right melancholy.

Would you bind them wrist to wrist--
  Foot to foot the truants shackle,
From your toils away they twist
  Into air with giddy cackle.

Crack of whip or edge of steel
  Cannot hold them in your keeping;
With the wriggle of an eel
  From your grasp they still go leaping.

Never yet was fetter found,
  Never lock contrived, to hold them;
Never dungeon underground,
  Moor or mountain keep controlled them.

Thou whose glance alone makes pure,
  Searcher of all hearts and Saviour,
With Thy Sevenfold Spirit cure
  My stray thoughts' unblessed behaviour.

God of earth, air, fire and flood,
  Rule me, rule me in such measure,
That to my eternal good
  I may live to love Thy pleasure.

Christ's own flock thus may I reach,
  At the flash of Death's sharp sickle,
Just in deed, of steadfast speech,
  Not, as now, infirm and fickle.

THE MONK AND HIS WHITE CAT

(After an eighth- or early ninth-century Irish poem. Text and translation in **Thesaurus Palaeohibernicus**.)

Pangar, my white cat, and I
  Silent ply our special crafts;
Hunting mice his one pursuit,
  Mine to shoot keen spirit shafts.

Rest, I love, all fame beyond,
  In the bond of some rare book;
Yet white Pangar from his play
  Casts, my way, no jealous look.

Thus alone within one cell
  Safe we dwell--not dull the tale--
Since his ever favourite sport
  Each to court will never fail.

Now a mouse, to swell his spoils,
  In his toils he spears with skill;
Now a meaning deeply thought
  I have caught with startled thrill.

Now his green full-shining gaze
  Darts its rays against the wall;
Now my feebler glances mark
  Through the dark bright knowledge fall.

Leaping up with joyful purr,
  In mouse fur his sharp claw sticks,
Problems difficult and dear,
  With my spear I, too, transfix.

Crossing not each other's will,
  Diverse still, yet still allied,
Following each his own lone ends,
  Constant friends we here abide.

Pangar, master of his art,
  Plays his part in pranksome youth;
While in age sedate I clear
  Shadows from the sphere of Truth.

A PRAYER TO THE VIRGIN

(Edited by Strachan in *Eriu*, vol. i, p. 122. Tenth or perhaps ninth century)

Gentle Mary, Noble Maiden,
Hearken to our suppliant pleas!
Shrine God's only Son was laid in!
Casket of the Mysteries!

Holy Maid, pure Queen of Heaven,
Intercession for us make,
That each hardened heart's transgression
May be pardoned for Thy sake.

Bent in loving pity o'er us,
Through the Holy Spirit's power,
Pray the King of Angels for us
In Thy Visitation hour.

Branch of Jesse's tree whose blossoms
Scent the heavenly hazel wood,
Pray for me for full purgation
Of my bosom's turpitude.

Mary, crown of splendour glowing,
Dear destroyer of Eve's ill,
Noble torch of Love far-showing,
Fruitful stock of God's good will;

Heavenly Virgin, Maid transcendent,
Yea! He willed that Thou shouldst be
His fair Ark of Life Resplendent,
His pure Queen of Chastity.

Mother of all good, to free me,
Interceding at my side,
Pray Thy First-Born to redeem me,
When the Judgment books are wide;

Star of knowledge, rare and noble,
Tree of many-blossoming sprays,
Lamp to light our night of trouble,
Sun to cheer our weary days;

Ladder to the Heavenly Highway,
Whither every Saint ascends,
Be a safeguard still, till my way
In Thy glorious Kingdom ends!

Covert fair of sweet protection,
Chosen for a Monarch's rest,
Hostel for nine months' refection
Of a Noble Infant Guest;

Glorious Heavenly Porch, whereunder,
So the day-star sinks his head,
God's Own Son--O saving wonder!
Jesus was incarnated;

For the fair Babe's sake conceived
In Thy womb and brought to birth,
For the Blest Child's sake, received

Now as King of Heaven and Earth;

For His Rood's sake! starker, steeper
Hath no other Cross been set,
For His Tomb's sake! darker, deeper
There hath been no burial yet;

By His Blessed Resurrection,
When He triumphed o'er the tomb,
By The Church of His affection
'During till the Day of Doom,

Safeguard our unblest behaviour,
Till behind Death's blinding veil,
Face to face, we see our Saviour.
This our prayer is: Hail! All Hail!

MAELISU'S HYMN TO THE ARCHANGEL MICHAEL

(By Maelisu ua Brochain, a writer of religious poetry both in Irish and Latin who died in 1051. Mael-Isu means "the tonsured of Jesus.")

Angel and Saint,
O Michael of the oracles,
O Michael of great miracles,
Bear to the Lord my plaint!

Hear my request!
Ask of the great, forgiving God,
To lift this vast and grievous load
Of sin from off my breast.

Why, Michael, tarry
My fervent prayer with upward wing
Unto the King, the great High King
Of Heaven and Earth, to carry?

Unto my soul
Bring help, bring comfort, yea bring power
To win release, in death's black hour,
From sin, distress, and dole.

Till, as devoutly
My fading eyes seek Heaven's dim height,
To meet me with thy myriads bright,
Do thou adventure stoutly.

Captain of hosts,
Against earth's wicked, crooked clan
To aid me lead thy battle van
And quell their cruel boasts.

Archangel glorious,
Disdain not now thy suppliant urgent,
But over every sin insurgent
Set me at last victorious.

Thou art my choosing!
That with my body, soul, and spirit
Eternal life I may inherit,
Thine aid be not refusing.

In my sore need
O thou of Anti-Christ the slayer,
Triumphant victor, to my prayer
Give heed, O now give heed!

MAELISU'S HYMN TO THE HOLY SPIRIT

O Holy Spirit, hasten to us!
Move round about us, in us, through us!
All our deadened souls' desires
Inflame anew with heavenly fires!

Yea! let each heart become a hostel

Of Thy bright Presence Pentecostal,
Whose power from pestilence and slaughter
Shall shield us still by land and water.

From bosom sins, seducing devils,
From Hell with all its hundred evils,
For Jesus' only sake and merit,
Preserve us, Thou Almighty Spirit!

EVE'S LAMENTATION

(From the Early Irish)

I am Eve, great Adam's wife,
'Twas my guilt took Jesus' life.
Since of Heaven I robbed my race,
On His Cross was my true place.

In His Paradise, God placed me,
Then a wicked choice disgraced me.
At the counsel of the Devil,
My pure hand I stained with evil;

For I put it forth and plucked,
Then the deadly apple sucked.
Long as woman looks on day,
Shall she walk in folly's way.

Winter's withering icy woe,
Whelming wave and smothering snow,
Hell to fright and death to grieve--
Had been never, but for Eve!

ALEXANDER THE GREAT

(From the Early Irish)

Four Sages stood to chant a stave
Above the proud Earth Conqueror's grave;
And all their words were words of candour
Above the urn of Alexander.

The first began: "But yesterday,
When all in state the Great King lay,
Myriads around him made their moan,
To-day he lieth all alone!"

"But yesterday," the second sang,
"O'er Earth his charger's hoof outrang;
To-day its outraged soil instead
Is riding heavy o'er his head!"

"But yesterday," the third went on,
"All Earth was swayed by Philip's son:
To-day, to shroud his calcined bones,
Seven feet thereof is all he owns!"

"But yesterday, so liberal he,
Silver and gold he scattered free;
To-day," the last outsighed his thought,
"His wealth abounds but he is naught!"

Thus sentence gave these Sages four,
Above the buried Emperor;
It was no foolish women's prate
That held them thus in high debate.

THE KINGS WHO CAME TO CHRIST

(From the Early Irish)

Three Kings came to the Babe's abode,
  With faces that like bright moons glowed,
From out the learned Eastern world,
  Where o'er wide plains slow streams are curled.

The three sought out the lovely Child,
  On whom, white-blossomed Bethel smiled,
Three, o'er all knowledge granted sway,
  Three Seers of the Vision they.

The Promise of the Great All-wise
  Was present to their prescient eyes,
A Vision beckoning from afar,
  The Christ Child cradled on a star;

A lofty star of lucent ray,
  It swam before them through the day,
And when earth's hues were lost in night,
  It still led on with loving light.

And still the lucky Royal Three
  Went following it full readily;
And still across the firmament
  An arch of blessed might it went.

So rushing radiant, round and soft,
  Past every star that paced aloft,
Right joyously it stayed for them
  At last o'er blessed Bethlehem.

O, then each Monarch of the Three
  With worship fell upon his knee,
And gave, while God he loud extolled,
  His frankincense and myrrh and gold.

They recognised the Babe's bright face
  And Mary in her Virgin grace.
'Twas thus the Star's Epiphany
  Showed Christ their King to the Kings three.

QUATRAINS

HOSPITALITY

Whether my house is dark or bright,
I close it not on any wight,
Lest Thou, hereafter, King of Stars,
Against me close Thy Heavenly bars.

If from a guest who shares thy board
Thy dearest dainty thou shalt hoard,
'Tis not that guest, O never doubt it,
But Mary's Son shall do without it.

THE BLACKBIRD

Ah, Blackbird, that at last art blest
 Because thy nest is on the bough,
No Hermit of the clinking bell,
How soft and well thy notes fall now.

MOLING SANG THIS

With the old when I consort
 Jest and sport they straight lay by;
When with frolic youth I am flung,
 Maddest of the young am I.

THE CHURCH BELL IN THE NIGHT

Sweet little bell, sweet little bell,
 Struck long and well upon the wind,
I'd rather tryst with thee to-night
 Than any maiden light of mind.

THE CRUCIFIXION

At the first bird's early crying,
They began Thy Crucifying,
O Thou of face as woeful wan,
As the far-flown winter swan.

Sore the suffering and the shame
Put upon Thy Sacred Frame;
Ah! but sorer the heartache
For Thy stricken Mother's sake.

THE PILGRIM AT ROME

Unto Rome wouldst thou attain,
Great the toil is, small the gain,
If the King thou seekest therein
Travel not, with thee, from Erin.

ON A DEAD SCHOLAR

Dead is Lon
  Of Kilgarrow,
  O great sorrow!
Dead and gone.
Dire the dolour,
  Erin, here and past thy border,
  Dire the dolour and disorder,
To the schools and to the scholar,
  Since our Lon
  Is dead and gone.

CHARMS AND INVOCATIONS

CHARMS AGAINST SORROW

A charm whereunto grief must yield--
The Charm of Michael with the Shield.

Charms before which all sorrows fail--
The Palm-branch of Christ and Brigit's Veil.

The charm Christ set for Himself, when the Godhead within Him darkened;
And when He cried from the Cross that His Father no longer hearkened.
When you are bound down by the Cross and night is blackest before you,
A charm that shall lift off sorrow's weight and to joyful hope restore you.
A charm to be said at sunrise when your hands your heart are crushing,
When the eyes are red with weeping and the madness of grief outrushing.
A charm with not even a whisper to spare,
But only the silent prayer.

ON COVERING THE FIRE FOR THE NIGHT

Let us preserve this seed of fire as Christ preserves us all,
Himself a-watch above the house, Bride at its middle wall,
Below the Twelve Apostles of highest heavenly sway,
Guarding and defending it until the dawn of day.

MORNING WISH

O Jesu! in the morning I cry and call thee early,
Blest only Son of God on high who purchased us so dearly.
O guard me in the shelter of Thy most Holy Cross,
All through the courses of the day keep me from sin and loss.

A CHARM AGAINST ENEMIES

Three powers are of the Evil One to curse mankind;
An Evil Eye, an Evil Tongue, an Evil Mind.
Three words are God's own breath and Mary's to her Son,
For she in heaven had heard them, told them every one.
The word of Mercy free, the singing word of Joy,
The binding word of Love He gives us to employ.
O may the saving might of these three holy words
On Erin's men and women light, and keep them still the Lord's.

CHARM FOR A PAIN IN THE HEART

"God save you my three brothers! God save you! Now how far
Have ye on foot to travel, by sun and moon and star?"

"To Olivet's own Mount we fare till we have gotten gold,
Therefrom a cup to fashion the tears of Christ to hold."

"So do! And when those Precious Tears drop down into the bowl
Into thy very heart they'll fall and cure thee body and soul."

THE SAFE-GUARDING OF MY SOUL

My succour from all sinful harms
  Be Thou, Almighty Father!
And Mary, who, within her arms
  The King of Kings did gather!
 And Michael, messenger to earth
  From out the Heavenly City,
 The Twelve of Apostolic worth,
  And last the Lord of Pity!
That so my soul, encircled by their care,
Into Heaven's Golden Halls with joy may fare!

THE WHITE PATERNOSTER.

On going to sleep, think that it is the sleep of Death and that you may be summoned to the Day of the Mountain of Judgment and say:

I lay me down with God;
  May He rest here also,
His Guardian arms around my head,
  Christ's Cross my limbs below.

Where wouldst, thou lay thee down?
  'Twixt Mary and her Son--
Brigit and her bright mantle,
Colomb and his shield handle,
God and His strong Right Hand.

At morn where wouldst thou rise?
With Patrick to the skies.

Lamentations

THE SONG OF CREDE, DAUGHTER OF GUARE

In the Battle of Aidne, Crede, the daughter of King Guare of Aidne,
beheld Dinertach of the HyFidgenti, who had come to the help of Guare
with seventeen wounds upon his breast. Then she fell in love with him.
He died and was buried in the cemetery of Colman's Church.

"These are the arrows that murder sleep,"
At every hour in the night's black deep;
Pangs of Love through the long day ache
All for the dead Dinertach's sake.

Great love of a hero from Roiny's plain
Has pierced me through with immortal pain,
Blasted my beauty and left me to blanch,
A riven bloom on a restless branch!

Never was song like Dinertach's speech,
But holy strains that to Heaven's gate reach.
A front of flame without boast or pride,
Yet a firm, fond mate for a fair maid's side.

A growing girl--I was timid of tongue,
And never trysted with gallants young,
But, since I won on into passionate age,
Fierce love-longings my heart engage.

I have every bounty that life could hold,
With Guare, arch-monarch of Aidne cold,
But fallen away from my haughty folk,
In Irluachair's field my heart lies broke.

There is chanting in glorious Aidne's meadow
Under St. Colman's Church's shadow;
A hero flame sinks into the tomb--
Dinertach, alas, my love and my doom!

Chaste Christ! that unto my life's last breath
I trysted with Sorrow and mate with Death;
At every hour of the night's black deep,
These are the arrows that murder sleep!

THE DESERTED HOME

(An eleventh-century poem)

Keenly cries the blackbird now;
  From the bough his nest is gone.
For his slaughtered mate and young
  Still his tongue talks on and on.

Such, alas! not long ago
  Was the woe my heart befell;
Therefore, wherefore thine so grieves
  It perceives, O bird, too well!

Poor heart burnt with grief within
  By the sin of that rash band!
Little could they guess thy care,
  Crying there, or understand.

From afar at thy clear call
  Fluttered all thy new-fledged brood.
Now thy nest of love lies hid
  Down amid the nettles rude.

In one day the herd-boy crew
  Careless slew thy fledgelings fine.
One the fate to thine and thee,
  One the fate to me and mine.

As thy mate upon the mead
  Chirruped, feeding at thy side,
Taken in their snaring strands,
  At the herd-boy's hands she died.

O Thou Framer of our fates,
  Not an equal lot have all!
Neighbour's wife and child are spared,
  Ours, as though uncared for, fall.

Fairy hosts with blasting death
  Breathed on mine a breath abhorred;
Bloodless though their evil ire,
  It was direr than the sword.

Woe our wife! and woe our young!
  Sorrow-wrung our hearts complain!
Of each fair and faithful one
  Tidings none or trace remain!

THE MOTHERS' LAMENT AT THE SLAUGHTER OF THE INNOCENTS

(Probably a poem of the eleventh century. It is written in Rosg metre, and was first published in *The Gaelic Journal*, May 1891.)

Then, as the executioner plucked her son from her breast, one of the women said:

  "Why are you tearing
    Away to his doom
  The child of my caring,
    The fruit of my womb.
  Till nine months were o'er,
  His burthen I bore,
  Then his pretty lips pressed
  The glad milk from my breast,
  And my whole heart he filled,
  And my whole life he thrilled.

  "All my strength dies;
  My tongue speechless lies;
  Darkened are my eyes;
  His breath was the breath of me;
  His death is the death of me!"

Then another woman said:

  "Tis my own son that from me you wring,
  I deceived not the King.
  But slay me, even me,
  And let my boy be.

A mother most hapless,
My bosom is sapless.
Mine eyes one tearful river,
My frame one fearful shiver,
My husband sonless ever,
And I a sonless wife
To live a death in life.
O, my son! O, God of Truth!
O, my unrewarded youth!
O, my birthless sicknesses,
Until doom without redress!
O, my bosom's silent nest!
O, the heart broke in my breast!"

Then said another woman:

"Murderers, obeying
  Herod's wicked willing,
One ye would be slaying,
  Many are ye killing.
Infants would ye smother?
  Ruffians ye have rather
  Wounded many a father,
Slaughtered many a mother.
Hell's black jaws your horrid deed is glutting,
Heaven's white gate against your black souls shutting.

"Ye are guilty of the Great Offence!
Ye have spilt the blood of innocence."

And yet another woman said:

"O Lord Christ come to me!

Nay, no longer tarry!
With my son, home to Thee
  My soul quickly carry!
O Mary great, O Mary mild,
  Of God's One Son the Mother,
What shall I do without my child,
  For I have now no other.
For Thy Son's sake my son they slew,
  Those murderers inhuman;
My sense and soul they slaughtered too,
  I am but a crazy woman.
Yea! after that most piteous slaughter,
When my babe's life ran out like water,
The heart within my bosom hath become
A clot of blood from this day till the Doom!"

THE KEENING OF MARY

Taken down by Patrick H. Pearse from Mary Clancy of Moycullen, who keened it with great horror in her voice, in a low sobbing recitative.

MARY. "O Peter, O Apostle, my bright Love, hast thou found him?"
  "M'ochon agus m'ochon, O!"

PETER. "Even now in the midst of His foemen I found Him."
  "M'ochon agus m'ochon, O!"

MARY. "Come hither, ye two Marys, and my bright love be keening."

"M'ochon agus m'ochon, O!"

THE TWO MARYS. "If His body be not with us, sure our keene had little
   meaning."
   "M'ochon agus m'ochon, O!"

MARY. "Who is yonder stately Man on the Tree His passion showing?"
   "M'ochon agus m'ochon, O!"

CHRIST. "O Mother, thine own son, can it be thou art not knowing."
   "M'ochon agus m'ochon, O!"

MARY. "And is that the little son whom nine months I was bearing?"
   "M'ochon agus m'ochon, O!"
   "And is that the little son in the stall I was caring?
   And is that the little son this Mary's breast was draining?"
   "M'ochon agus m'ochon, O!"

CHRIST. "Hush thee, hush thee, Mother, and be not so complaining."

MARY. "And is this the very hammer that struck the sharp nails thro' thee?"
   "M'ochon agus m'ochon, O!"
   "And this the very spear that thy white side pierced and slew thee?"
   "M'ochon agus m'ochon, O!"
   "And is that the crown of thorns that thy beauteous head is caging?"
   "M'ochon agus m'ochon, O!"

CHRIST. "Hush, Mother, for my sake thy sorrow be assuaging."
   "M'ochon agus m'ochon, O!"
   "For thy own love's sake thy cruel sorrow smother!"
   "M'ochon agus m'ochon, O!"
   "The women of my keening are unborn yet, little Mother!"
   "M'ochon agus m'ochon, O!"

"O woman, why weepest thou my death that leads to pardon?"
"M'ochon agus m'ochon, O!"
"Happy hundreds, to-day, shall stray through Paradise Garden."
"M'ochon agus m'ochon, O!"

CAOINE

(From the eighteenth-century Irish)

Cold, dark, and dumb lies my boy on his bed;
Cold, dark, and silent the night dews are shed;
Hot, swift, and fierce fall my tears for the dead!

His footprints lay light in the dew of the dawn
As the straight, slender track of the young mountain fawn;
But I'll ne'er again follow them over the lawn.

His manly cheek blushed with the sun's rising ray,
And he shone in his strength like the sun at midday;
But a cloud of black darkness has hid him away.

And that black cloud for ever shall cling to the skies:
And never, ah, never, I'll see him arise,
Lost warmth of my bosom, lost light of my eyes!

Songs to Music

BATTLE HYMN

(Written to an old Irish Air)

Above the thunder crashes,
Around the lightning flashes:
Our heads are heaped with ashes
  But Thou, God, art nigh!
Thou launchest forth the levin,
The storm by Thee is driven,
Give heed, O Lord, from Heaven,
  Hear, hear our cry!

For lo, the Dane defaces
With fire Thy holy places,
He hews Thy priests in pieces,
  Our maids more than die.
Up, Lord, with storm and thunder,
Pursue him with his plunder,
And smite his ships in sunder,
  Lord God Most High!

THE SONG OF THE WOODS

(To an Irish Air of the same name)

Not only where Thy blessed bells
   Peal afar for praise and prayer,
Or where Thy solemn organ swells,
   Lord, not only art Thou there.
Thy voice of many waters
   From out the ocean comfort speaks,
Thy Presence to a radiant rose
   Thrills a thousand virgin peaks.

And here, where in one wondrous woof--
   Aisle on aisle and choir on choir--
To rear Thy rarest temple roof,
   Pillared oak and pine aspire;
Life-weary here we wander,
   When lo! the Saviour's gleaming stole!
'Tis caught unto our craving lips,
   Kissed and straightway we are whole.

THE ENCHANTED VALLEY

(To an Irish Air of the same name)

I will go where lilies blow
  Beside the flow of languid streams,
Within that vale of opal glow,
Where bright-winged dreams flutter to and fro,
  Fain am I its magic peace to know.

Beware! beware of that valley fair!
  All dwellers there to phantoms turn,
For joys and griefs they have none to share,
Tho' ever they yearn life's burdens to bear,
  Ah! of that valley beware, beware!

REMEMBER THE POOR

(Founded on an Irish Ballad of the name)

Oh! remember the poor when your fortune is sure,
  And acre to acre you join;
Oh! remember the poor, though but slender your store
  And you ne'er can go gallant and fine.
Oh! remember the poor when they cry at your door
  In the raging rain and blast;

Call them in! Cheer them up with the bite and the sup,
  Till they leave you their blessing at last.

The red fox has his lair, and each bird of the air
  With the night settles warm in his nest,
But the King Who laid down His celestial crown
  For our sakes--He had nowhere to rest.
Oh! the poor were forgot till their pitiful lot
  He bowed Himself to endure;
If your souls ye would make, for His Heavenly sake,
  Oh! remember, remember the poor.

II. WELSH POEMS

THE ODES TO THE MONTHS

(After Aneurin, a sixth-century warrior bard)

Month of Janus, the coom is smoke-fuming;
Weary the wine-bearer; minstrels far roaming;
Lean are the kine; the bees never humming;
Milking-folds void; to the kiln no meat coming;
Gaunt every steed; no pert sparrows strumming;
Long the night till the dawn; but a glimpse is the gloaming.
Sapient Cynfelyn, this was thy summing;
"Prudence is Man's surest guide, by my dooming."

*   *   *   *   *

Month of Mars; the birds become bolder;
Wounding the wind upon the cape's shoulder;
Serene skies delay till the young crops are older;
Anger burns on, when grief waxes colder;
Every man's mind some dread may unsolder;
Each bird wins the may that hath long been a scolder;

Each seed cleaves the clay, though for long months amoulder,
Yet the dead still must stay in the tomb, their strong holder.

* * * * *

Month of Augustus--the beach is a-spray;
Blithesome the bee and the hive full alway;
Better work than the bow hath the sickle to-day;
Fuller the stack than the House of the Play;
The Churl who cares neither to work nor to pray
Now why should he cumber the earth with his clay?
Justly St. Breda, the sapient, would say
"As many to evil as good take the way."

* * * * *

Month of September--benign planets shiver;
Serene round the hamlet are ocean and river;
Not easy for men and for steeds is endeavour;
Trees full of fruit, as of arrows the quiver.
A Princess was born to us, blessed for ever,
From slavery's shackles our land's freedom-giver.
Saith St. Berned the Saint, ripe Wisdom's mouth ever;
"In sleep shall God nod, Who hath sworn to deliver?"

Month of October--thin the shade is showing;
Yellow are the birch-trees; bothies empty growing;
Full of flesh, bird and fish to the market going;
Less and less the milk now of cow and goat is flowing,
Alas! for him who meriteth disgrace by evil-doing;
Death is better far than extravagance's strowing.
Three acts should follow crime, to true repentance owing--

Fasting and prayer and of alms abundance glowing.

*　　*　　*　　*　　*

Month of December--with mud the shoe bemired;
Heavy the land, the sun in heaven tired;
Bare all the trees, little force now required;
Cheerful the cock; by dark the thief inspired.

Whilst the Twelve Months thus trip in dance untired,
Round youthful minds Satan still weaves his fetter.
Justly spake Yscolan, Wisdom's sage begetter,
"Than an evil prophecy God is ever better."

THE TERCETS

(After Llywarch Hen, a sixth-century prince and poet)

Set is the snare, the ash clusters glow,
Ducks plash in the pools; breakers whiten below;
More strong than a hundred is the heart's hidden woe.

Long is the night; resounding the shore,
Frequent in crowds a tumultuous roar,
The evil and good disagree evermore.

Long is the night; the hill full of cries;
O'er the tree-tops the wind whistles and sighs,

Ill nature deceives not the wit of the wise.

The greening birch saplings asway in the air
Shall deliver my feet from the enemy's snare.
It is ill with a youth thy heart's secrets to share.

The saplings of oak in yonder green glade
Shall loosen the snare by an enemy laid.
It is ill to unbosom thy heart to a maid.

The saplings of oak in their full summer pride
Shall loosen the snare by the enemy tied.
It is ill to a babbler thy heart to confide.

The brambles with berries of purple are dressed;
In silence the brooding thrush clings to her nest,
In silence the liar can never take rest.

Rain is without--wet the fern plume;
White the sea gravel--fierce the waves spume.
There is no lamp like reason man's life to illume.

Rain is without, but the shelter is near;
Yellow the furze, the cow-parsnip is sere,
God in Heaven, how couldst Thou create cowards here!

HAIL, GLORIOUS LORD!

(From a twelfth-century MS., "The Black Book of Carmarthen")

Hail, all glorious Lord! with holy mirth
May Church and chancel bless Thy good counsel!
Each chancel and church,
All plains and mountains,
And ye three fountains--
Two above wind,
  And one above earth!
May light and darkness bless Thee!
Fine silk, green forest confess Thee!
Thus did Abraham father
Of faith with joy possess Thee.
Bird and bee-song bless Thee,
  Among the lilies and roses!
All the old, all the young
Laud thee with joyful tongue,
As Thy praise was once sung
  By Aaron and Moses.
Male and female,
The days that are seven,
The stars of heaven,
The air and the ether,
Every book and fair letter;
Fish in waters fair-flowing,
And song and deed glowing!
Grey sand and green sward
Make your blessing's award!
And all such as with good

Have satisfied stood!
While my own mouth shall bless Thee
And my Saviour confess Thee.
  Hail, glorious Lord!

MY BURIAL

(After Dafydd ab Gwilym, the most famous Welsh lyrical poet, 1340-1400)

When I die, O, bury me
  Within the free young wild wood;
Little birches, o'er me bent,
  Lamenting as my child would!
Let my surplice-shroud be spun
  Of sparkling summer clover;
While the great and stately treen
  Their rich rood-screen hang over!
For my bier-cloth blossomed may
  Outlay on eight green willows!
Sea-gulls white to bear my pall
  Take flight from all the billows.
Summer's cloister be my church
  Of soft leaf-searching whispers,
From whose mossed bench the nightingale
  To all the vale chants vespers!
Mellow-toned, the brake amid,
  My organ hid be cuckoo!
Paters, seemly hours and psalm

Bird voices calm re-echo!
Mystic masses, sweet addresses,
  Blackbird, be thou offering;
Till God His Bard to Paradise
  Uplift from sighs and suffering.

THE LAST CYWYDD

(After Dafydd ab Gwilym)

Memories fierce like arrows pierce;
  Alone I waste and languish,
And make my cry to God on high
  To ease me of mine anguish.
If heroic was my youth,
  In truth its powers are over;
With brain dead and force sped,
  Love sets at naught the lover!
The Muse from off my lips is thrust,
  'Tis long since song has cheered me;
Gone is Ivor, counsellor just,
  And Nest, whose grace upreared me!
Morfydd, all my world and more,
  Lies low in churchyard gravel;
While beneath the burthen frore
  Of age alone I travel.

Mute, mute my song's salute,

When summer's beauties thicken;
Cuckoo, nightingale, no art
  Of yours my heart can quicken!
Morfydd, not thy haunting kiss
  Or voice of bliss can save me
From the spear of age whose chill
  Has quenched the thrill love gave me.
My ripe grain of heart and brain
  The sod sadly streweth;
Its empty chaff with mocking laugh
  The wind of death pursueth!
Dig my grave! O, dig it deep
  To hide my sleeping body,
So but Christ my spirit keep,
  Amen! ab Gwilym's ready!

THE LABOURER

(After Iolo Goch, "Iowerlt the Red," a fourteenth-century bard and son
of the Countess of Lincoln)

When the folk of all the Earth,
For the weighing of their worth,
Promised by his Ancient Word,
Freely flock before The Lord--
And His Judgment-seat is set
High on mighty Olivet,
Forthright then shall be the tale

Of the Plougher of the Vale,
If so be his tithes were given
Justly to the King of Heaven;
If he freely shared his store
With the sick or homeless poor--
When his soul is at God's feet
Rich remembrance it shall meet.

He who turns and tills the sod
Leans by Nature on his God.
Save his plough-beam naught he judgeth,
None he angereth, or grudgeth,
Strives with none, takes none in toils,
Crushes none and none despoils;
Overbeareth not, though strong,
Doth not even a little wrong.

"Suffering here," he saith, "is meet,
Else were Heaven not half so sweet."
Following after goad and plough,
With unruffled breast and brow,
Is to him an hundred-fold
Dearer than, for treasured gold,
Even in King Arthur's form,
Castles to besiege and storm.

If the labourer were sped,
Where would be Christ's Wine and Bread?
Certes but for his supply,
Pope and Emperor must die,
Every wine-free King and just,
Yea! each mortal turn to dust.

Blest indeed is he whose hands
Steer the plough o'er stubborn lands.
How through far-spread broom and heath
Tear his sharp, smooth coulter's teeth--
Old-time relic, heron-bill,
Rooting out fresh furrows still,
With a noble, skilful grace
Smoothing all the wild land's face,
Reaching out a stern, stiff neck
Each resisting root to wreck.

*   *   *   *   *

Behind his oxen on his path
Thus he strides the healthy strath,
Chanting many a godly rhyme
To the plough-chain's silver chime.
All the crafts that ever were
With the Ploughman's ill compare.
Ploughing, in an artful wise,
Earth's subduing signifies,
Far as Baptism and Creed,
Far as Christendom hath speed.

By God, who is man's Master best,
And Mary may the plough be blest.

THE ELEGY ON SION GLYN, A CHILD OF FIVE YEARS OF AGE

(By his Father, Lewis Glyn Cothi, 1425-1486)

One wee son, woe worth his sire!
My treasure was and heart's desire;
But evermore I now must pine,
Mourning for that wee son of mine,
Sick to the heart, day out and in,
Thinking and thinking of Johnny Glynn,
My fairy prince for ever fled,
Leaving life's Mabinogion dead.

A rosy apple, pebbles white,
And dicky-birds were his delight,
A childish bow with coloured cord,
A little brittle wooden sword.
From bagpipes or the bogy-man
Into his mother's arms he ran,
There coaxed from her a ball to throw
With his daddy to and fro.

His own sweet songs he'd then be singing,
Then for a nut with a shout be springing;
Holding my hand he'd trot about with me,
Coax me now, and now fall out with me,
Now, make it up again, lip to lip,
For a dainty die or a curling chip.
Would God my lovely little lad
A second life, like Lazarus, had!
St. Beuno raised from death at once

St. Winifred and her six nuns;
Would to God the Saint could win
An eighth from death in Johnny Glynn!

Ah, Mary! my merry little knave,
Coffined and covered in the grave!
To think of him beneath the slab
Deals my lone heart a double stab.

Bright dream beyond my own life's shore,
Proud purpose of my future's store,
My hope, my comfort from annoy,
My jewel and my glowing joy,
My nest of shade from out the sun,
My lark, my soaring, singing one,
My golden shaft of faithful love
Shot at the radiant round above,
My intercessor with Heaven's King,
My boyhood's second blossoming,
My little, laughing, loving John,
For you I'm sunk in shadow wan!

Good-bye, good-bye, for evermore
My little lively squirrel's store,
The happy bouncing of his ball,
His carol up and down the hall!
Adieu, my little dancing one,
Adieu, adieu, my son, my son!

THE NOBLE'S GRAVE

(After Sion Cent, 1386-1420, priest of Kentchurch, in Hereford)

Premier Peer but yesterday,
  Lone within the tomb to-morrow;
For his silken garments gay,
  Grave-clothes in a gravelled furrow.

No love-making, homage none;
  From his mines no golden mintage;
No rich traffic in the sun;
  No more purple-purling vintage.

No more usherings out of Hall
  By obsequious attendant;
No more part, however small,
  In the Pageant's pomp resplendent!

Just a perch of churchyard clay
  All the soil he now possesses;
Heavily its burthen grey
  On his pulseless bosom presses.

THE BARD'S DEATH-BED CONFESSION

(After Huw Morus, 1622-1709, a Welsh Cavalier poet)

Lord, hear my confession of life-long transgression!
  Weak-willed and too filled with Earth's follies am I
To reach by the strait way of faith to Heaven's gateway,
If Thou light not thither my late way.

From Duty's hard high road by Beauty's soft by-road
  To Satan's, not Thy road, I wandered away.
Thou hast seen, Father tender, Thou seest what a slender
Return for Thy Talents I render.

Thy pure Eyes pierced through me and probed me and knew me,
  Not flawless but lawless, when put to the proof.
In ease or in cumber, day-doings or slumber,
What ills of mine wouldst Thou not number!

From Thy Holy Hand's Healing, contrition annealing
  And Faith's oil of healing grant, Lord, I beseech;
These only can cure me and fresh life assure me,
These only Thy Peace can procure me!

To the blood freely flowing of The Lamb life-bestowing
  This wonder is owing that washes out sin;
Thy Love to us lent Him, Thy Love to death sent Him,
That man through Thy Love should repent him.

Lord God, Thy Protection, Lord Christ, Thy Affection,
  Holy Ghost, Thy Direction so govern my heart,

That all promptings other than Love's it may smother,
As a babe is subdued to its mother.

For that treasure of treasures that all price outmeasures,
　Pure Faith, on whose pleasures life-giving we feed--
Let Kings in their places, let all the earth's races
Sing aloud in a crowd of glad faces.

Yea! all mouths shall bless Thee, all hearts shall confess Thee
　The bounteous Fountain of mercy and love;
Each gift we inherit of pure, perfect merit,
Dear God, overflows from Thy Spirit.

QUICK, DEATH!

(After Huw Morus)

This room an antechamber is:
Beyond--the Hall of Very Bliss!
Quick, Death! for underneath thy door
I see the glimmering of Heaven's floor.

COUNSEL IN VIEW OF DEATH

(After Elis Wyn, 1671-1734, one of the Welsh Classics)

Leave your land, your goods lay down!
Life's green tree shall soon grow brown.
Pride of birth and pleasure gay
Renounce or they shall own you!

Manly strength and beauty fair,
Dear-bought sense, experience rare,
Learning ripe, companions fond
Yield, lest their bond ensnare you!

Is there then no sure relief,
Thou arch-murderer and thief,
Death, from thine o'ermastering law--
Thy monstrous maw can none shun?

O ye rich, in all your pride
Through the ages would ye bide,
Wherefore not with Death compound,
Ere underground he hide you?

Lusty athlete, light of foot,
Death, the Bowman's fell pursuit
Challenge! O, the laurels won,
If thou but shun his shooting!

Travellers by sea and land
On remotest mount or strand,

Have ye found one secret spot
Where Death is not commanding?

Learned scholar, jurist proud,
Lifted god-like o'er the crowd,
Can your keenest counsel's aid
Dispel Death's shade enshrouding?

Fervent faith, profound repentance,
Holy hours of stern self-sentence--
These alone can victory bring
When Death's dread sting shall wring us.

FROM "THE LAST JUDGMENT"

(After Goronwy Owen, 1728-1769, next to Dafydd ab Gwilym, the greatest
poet who sang in the old Welsh metres)

Day of Doom, at thy glooming
  May Earth be but meet for thee!
Day, whose hour of louring
  Not angels in light foresee!
To Christ alone and the Father
  'Tis known when thy hosts of might
Swift as giants shall gather,
  Yet stealthy as thieves at night.

Then what woe to the froward,
  What joy to the just and kind!
When the Seraph band comes streaming
  Christ's gleaming banner behind;
Heavenly blue shall its hue be
  To a myriad marvelling eyes;
Save where its heart encrimsons
  The cross of the sacrifice!

Rocks in that day's black fury
  Like leaves shall be whirled in the blast;
Hoary-headed Eryri
  Prone to the plough-lands cast!
Then shall be roaring and warring
  And ferment of sea and firth,
Ocean, in turmoil upboiling,
  Confounding each bound of earth.
The flow of the Deluge of Noah
  Were naught by that fell Flood's girth!

Then Heaven's pure self shall offer
  Her multitudinous eyes,
Cruel blinding to suffer,
  As her sun faints out of the skies;
And the bright-faced Moon shall languish
  And perish in such fierce pain
As darkened and shook with anguish
  All Life, when the Lamb was slain.

A GOOD WIFE

(After the Vicar Pritchard, 1569-1644)

Wise yokel foolish King excelleth;
Good name than spikenard sweeter smelleth!
What's gold to prudence? Strength to grace?
Man's more than goods; God first in place.

What though her dowry be but meagre,
Far better wise, God-fearing Igir,
Than yonder vain and brainless doll,
Helpless her fortune to control.

A wife that's true and kind and sunny
Is better than a mint of money;
Better than houses, land and gold
Or pearls and gems to have and hold.

A ship is she with jewels freighted,
Her price beyond all rubies rated,
A hundred-virtued amulet
To such as her in marriage get.

Gold pillar to a silver socket;
The weakling's tower of strength, firm-locked,
The very golden crown of life;
Grace upon grace--a virtuous wife.

"MARCHOG JESU!"

(Hymn sung at the Investiture of the Prince of Wales, the Welsh words by Pantycelyn, the famous eighteenth-century hymn-writer)

Lord, ride on in triumph glorious,
  Gird Thy sword upon Thy Thigh!
Earth shall own Thy Might Victorious,
  Death and Hell confounded lie.
Yea! before Thine Eye all-seeing,
  All Thy foes shall fly aghast;
Nature's self, through all her being,
  Tremble at Thy Trampling Past.

Pierce, for Thou alone art able,
  Pierce our dungeon with Thy day;
Shatter all the gates of Babel,
  Rend her iron bars away!
Till, as billows thunder shoreward,
  All the Ransomed Ones ascend,
Into freedom surging forward
  Without number, without end.

Who are these whose praises pealing
  From beyond the Morning Star
Earthward solemnly are stealing
  Down the distance faint and far?
These are they, the Ever Living,
  All in glistening garments gone,
Palm in hand, with proud Thanksgiving
  Up before the Great White Throne.

THE DESTRUCTION OF JERUSALEM

(After Eben Fardd, 1802-1863, one of the leading Welsh poets of the nineteenth century)

RACHEL MOURNING

Rachel, ah me! most wretchedly
  Mourns, meekest, worthiest woman,
Her husband dear hurled to his bier
  By Roman fiends inhuman.
Tremulously now murmurs she:
  "Naught's here but naked horror;
Black despond and blind despair,
  Mad turmoil, murderous terror!
Free he rose, his hero blows
  Gave Rome black cause to rue him;
Ten to one, then they run
  Their poisonous poignards through him.
Thus took flight thy tortured sprite,
  Dear heart, from my fond seeing!
Now stars on high in stark dawn die,
  We too must far be fleeing.
Children dear, I thrill with fear
  To hear your hungry crying!
Away, away! one more such day--
  And we're too weak for flying."

THE BURNING TEMPLE

The savage foes of this lost land of ours
Conspire to fire Antonius' shapely towers.
Ere long the Temple proud, surpassing all
Art's fairest gems, shall unto earth be bowed!
Lo! through the lurid gloom the lightning's lash!
And hark the unnatural thunder crash and boom!
Moriah's marvellous fane is leaning low;
With cries of woe her rafters rend in twain;
For our Imperial One is brought to naught.
Yea, even where most cunningly she was wrought,
The fire has cleft its way each coign into,
For wood and stone searching her bosom through.
Astonishingly high she took the blue,
Yet weeping molten dross shall meet the ground--
A sight for grief profound to gaze across.
Flame follows flame, each like a giant worm,
To feast and batten on her beauteous form.
Through gold and silver doors they sinuous swarm
And crop the carven flowers with gust enorme;
Till all is emptiness.
                    Then with hellish shout
The embruted Gentiles in exultant rout
Into her Holy of Holies profanely press!

One streaming flood of steaming blood--
   Shudders her sacred pavement!

LOVE DIVINE

(From "Emanuel." After Gwilym Hiraethog, 1802-1880.)

When the angel trumpet sounded.
  Through the unbounded ether blown,
Star on star danced on untiring,
  Choiring past the Great White Throne;
Then as, every globe outglancing,
  Earth's entrancing orb went by,
Love Divine in blushing pleasure
  Steeped the azure of the sky.

Wisdom, when she saw Earth singled
  From the bright commingled band,
Whispered Mercy: "That green wonder
  Yonder is thy promised land!"
Mercy looked and loved Earth straightway,
  At Heaven's gateway smiling set.
Ah! that glance of tender yearning
  She is turning earthward yet.

BEHIND THE VEIL

(After Islwyn, 1832-1878, the Welsh Wordsworth)

What say ye, can we charge a master soul
With error, when beyond all life's experience
Between the cradle and the grave, it rises,
Whispering of things unutterable, breaks its bond
With outward sense and sinks into itself,
As fades a star in space? Hath not that soul
A history in itself, a refluent tide
Of mystery murmuring out of unplumbed deeps,
On distant inaccessible strands, whereon
Memory lies dead amid the monstrous wreckage
Of jarring worlds? Are yonder stars above
As spiritually, magnificently bright
As Poesy feigns? May not some slumbering sense,
A memory dim of those diviner days,
When all the Heavens were yet aglow with God,
Transfuse them through and through with glimmering grace
And glory? Still the Stars within us shine,
And Poesy is but a recollection
Of Something greater gone, a presage proud
Of Something greater yet to be. What soul
But sometimes thrills with hauntings of a world
For long forgotten, at a glimpse begotten
Once more, then gone again? Imaginations?
Nay why not memories of a life than ours
A thousand times more blest within us buried
So deeply, the divine all-searching breath
Of Poesy alone can lure it forth.

All hail that hour when God's Redeeming Face
Shall so illume our past existences,
That through them all man's spirit shall see plain,
And to his blessed past relink Life's broken chain.

THE REIGN OF LOVE

(After Ceiriog, to a Welsh Air. Ceiriog, 1832-1887, was the Welsh Burns;
his songs to old Welsh Airs are the best of their kind.)

Love that invites, love that delights,
From hedgerow lush and leafy heights
  Is flooding all the air;
Their forest harps the breezes strum,
The happy brooks their burden hum;
There's nothing deaf, there's nothing dumb,
  But music everywhere!

Above the airy steep
Their lyres of gold the angels sweep,
Glad holiday with earth to keep
  Before the Great White Throne.
Then, when Heaven and earth and sea
Are joining in Love's jubilee;
While morning stars make melody,
  Shall man be mute alone?

Naught that hath birth matches the worth
Of Love, in God's own Heaven and Earth,
  For through His power divine
Love opes the golden eye of day,
Love guides the pale moon's lonely way,
Love lights the glow-worm's glimmering ray
  Amid the darkling bine.

Heavenly hue and form
Above, around, are glowing warm,
From His right hand Who rides the storm,
  Yet paints the lily's cheek.
Yea! whereso'er man lifts his eyes
To wood or wave or sunset skies,
A myriad magic shapes arise
  Eternal Love to speak.

PLAS GOGERDDAN

(After Ceiriog to a Welsh Air)

"Without thy Sire hast thou returned?"
  In grief the Princess cried!
"Go back!--or from my sight be spurned--
  To battle by his side.
I gave thee birth; but struck to earth
  I'd sooner see thee lie,
Or on thy bier come carried here,

Than thus a craven fly!

"Seek yonder hall, and pore on all
  The portraits of thy race;
The courage high that fires each eye
  Canst thou endure to face?"
"I'll bring no blame on thy fair name,
  Or my forefathers slight!
But kiss and bless me, mother dear,
  Ere I return to fight."

He fought and fell--his stricken corse
  They bore to her abode;
"My son!" she shrieked, in wild remorse;
  "Forgive me, O! my God!"
Then from the wall old voices fall:
  "Rejoice for such a son!
His deed and thine shall deathless shine,
  Whilst Gwalia's waters run!"

ALL THROUGH THE NIGHT

Ar Hyd y Nos

(After Ceiriog to this Welsh Air)

Fiery day is ever mocking
  Man's feeble sight;

Darkness eve by eve unlocking
  Heav'n's casket bright;
Thence the burdened spirit borrows
Strength to meet laborious morrows,
Starry peace to soothe his sorrows,
  All through the night.

Planet after planet sparkling,
  All through the night,
Down on Earth, their sister darkling,
  Shed faithful light.
In our mortal day's declining,
May our souls, as calmly shining,
Cheer the restless and repining,
  Till lost in sight.

DAVID OF THE WHITE ROCK

Dafydd y Garreg Wen

(After Ceiriog to this Welsh Air)

"All my powers wither,
  Death presses me hard;
Bear my harp hither!"
  Sighed David the Bard.

"Thus while life lingers,

In one lofty strain
O, let my fond fingers
  Awake it again.

"Last night an angel
  Cried, 'David, come sound
Christ's dear Evangel
  Death's valley around!'"

Wife and child harkened
  His harp's solemn swell;
Till his eye darkened,
  And lifeless he fell.

THE HIGH TIDE

(After Elvet Lewis, a contemporary Welsh poet)

A balmy air blows; the waterflags shiver,
On, on the Tide flows, on, on, up the river!

To no earth or sky allegiance he oweth;
He comes, who knows why? unless the Moon knoweth.

The Tide flows and flows; by hill and by hollow,
White rose upon rose, the foam flowers follow.

He spreads broad and full from margent to margent,
The wings of the gull are his bannerets argent.

The Tide flows and flows; Atlantic's loud charges
Mix in murmurous close with the wash of the barges.

With wondering ear the children cease playing;
The voice that they hear, what can it be saying?

Too well they shall know, when amid the wild brattle
Of the waters below, they enter life's battle.

The Tide flows apace; the ship that lies idle
Trips out with trim grace, like a bride to her bridal.

What hath she in store? shall Fate her boon give her?
Or must she no more return to the river?

The flood has gone past! Ah me! one was late for it,
And friends cry aghast: "How long must he wait for it?"

Young eyes that to-night are darkened for sorrow
Shall hail with delight their dear ship to-morrow.

Amid the sea-wrack the barque, tempest battered,
At length staggers back, like a prodigal tattered!

What if she be scarred or scoffers make light of her?
Though blemished and marred, how blest is the sight of her!

The Tide flows and flows, far past the grey towers;
And whispering goes through the wheat and the flowers.

And now his pulse takes the calm heart of the valley
And lifts, till it shakes, the low bough of the sally.

Slow, and more slow is his flow--he has tarried--
The blue Ocean's pilgrim, outwearied, miscarried!

Far, far from home, in wandering error,
A dim rocky dome beshrouding his mirror.

But hark! a voice thrills the traveller erring;
In the heart of the hills its sea-call is stirring:

And home, ever home, to its passionate pleading,
One whirl of white foam, with the ebb he is speeding.

"ORA PRO NOBIS"

(After Eifion Win, 1867- . He lies as a poet between Elfed and the "New
Bards")

A sudden shower lashes
  The darkening pane;
The voice of the tempest
  Is lifted again.
The centuried oaks
  To their very roots rock;
And crying, for shelter
  Course cattle and flock.

Our Father, forget not
  The nestless bird now;
The snow is so near,
  And so bare is the bough!

A great flood is flashing
  Athwart the wide lee;
Like a storm-struck encampment,
  The clouds rend and flee;
At the scourge of the storm
  My cot quakes with affright;
Far better the hearth
  Than the pavement to-night!
Our Father, forget not
  The homeless outcast;
So thin is his raiment,
  So bitter Thy blast!

The foam-flakes are whirling
  Below on the strand,
As white as the pages
  I turn with my hand;
And the curlew afar,
  From his storm-troubled lair,
Laments with the cry
  Of a soul in despair.
Our Father, forget not
  Our mariners' state;
Their ships are so slender,
  Thy seas are so great.

A FLOWER-SUNDAY LULLABY

(After Eifion Win, the contemporary Welsh poet)

Though the blue slab hides our laddy,
   Slumber, free of fear!
Well we know it, I and daddy,
   Naught can harm you here.
You and all the little sleepers,
   Their small graves within,
Have bright angels for door-keepers.
   Sleep, Goronwy Wyn!

Ah, too well I now remember,
   Darling, when you slept,
How the children from your chamber
   Jealously I kept.
Now how willingly to wake you
   I would let them in,
If their merry noise could make you
   Move, Goronwy Wyn!

Sleep, though mother is not near you,
   In God's garden green!
Flower-Sunday gifts we bear you,
   Lovely to be seen;
Six small primroses to show us
   Summer-time is ours;
Though, alas! locked up below us,
   Lies our flower of flowers.

Sleep! to mother's love what matters
  Passing time or tide?
On my ear your footstep patters,
  Still my babe you bide.
All the others moving, moving,
  Still disturb my breast;
But the dead have done with roving,
  You alone have rest.

Then, beneath the primrose petals,
  Sleep, our heart's delight!
Darkness o'er us deeply settles;
  We must say "Good night!"
Your new cradle needs no shaking
  On its quiet floor.
Sleep, my child! till you are waking
  In my arms once more.

THE BALLAD OF THE OLD BACHELOR OF TY'N Y MYNYDD

(After W.J. Gruffydd, 1880- , one of the leading "New Bards")

Strongest swept his sickle through the whin-bush,
  Straightest down the ridge his furrows sped;
Early on the mountain ranged his reapers,
  Above his mattock late he bowed his head.

Love's celestial rapture once he tasted,
  Then a cloud of suffering o'er him crept.
Out along the uplands, in the dew-fall,
  He mourned the maid who in the churchyard slept,

With the poor he shared his scanty earnings,
  To the Lord his laden heart he breathed;
On his rustic heart fell two worlds' sunshine,
  And two worlds' blossoms round his footsteps wreathed.

Much he gloried in Young Gwalia's doings,
  Yet more dearly loved her early lore,
Catching ever from her Triple Harpstrings
  The far, faint echoes of her ancient shore.

Yestereven he hung up his sickle,
  Ne'er again to trudge his grey fields o'er,
Ne'er again to plough the stony ridges,
  To sow the home of thorns, alas! no more.

THE QUEEN'S DREAM

(To a Welsh Air of the name)

From the starving City
  She turned her couch to seek,
With pearls of tender pity
  On her queenly cheek;

There in restless slumber
  She dreamt that she was one
Of that most piteous number
  By distress undone.
In among that sullen brood,
  In homeless want she glided,
While in mock solicitude
  Her fate they thus derided:
"Queen, now bear thee queenly,
  In destiny's despite!
If ***thou*** wilt starve serenely,
  We poor wretches might."

But, amid their mocking,
  "The King, the King!" they cry,
And forward they run flocking
  While He passes by;
With the crowd she mixes
  Her cruel shame to hide;
When, O, what wonder fixes
  The surging human tide?
There One stood, with thorn-crown'd head,
  Hands of supplication,
Multiplying mystic bread
  For her famished nation.
"Children thus remember
  My poor and Me!" He spoke,
And in her palace chamber
  Weeping she awoke.

THE WELSH FISHERMEN

(To the air of "The Song of the Bottle")

Up, up with the anchor,
  Round, round for the harbour mouth!
Wind, boys, and a spanker
  Racing due south!
Where 'ood you be going?
  How, now can ye hoist your sails?
When blossoms be blowing
  Over Welsh Wales!
Dear hearts for the herring,
Sure, after the herring,
Hot after the herring,
  Each ship of us sails.
Up, up with the anchor,
  Round, round for the harbour mouth!
Wind boys and a spanker,
  Racing due south.

"Men, when you go rocking,
  Out under the angry gale,
Wives' hearts begin knocking,
  Lasses turn pale.
Oh, why start a-fishing
  Far, far and across the foam?
Give way to our wishing;
  Stay, stay at home!"
"Now, but for King Herring,
  What 'ood you be wearing,

How 'ood you be faring
  How keep ye warm?
Lest loaves should be failing,
  Lest children for want take harm,
Men still will go sailing
  Out into the storm."

Then men, since it must be,
  Then men, since it must be so,
Christ, Christ shall our trust be,
  When the winds blow.
Once when He was sleeping,
  "Save Lord!" the disciples cried,
"Wild waters are leaping
  Over the side!"
See He has awoken!
  Hark, hark, He has spoken,
"Peace, peace," and in token
  Down the storm died.
Lord God of the billows,
  Still succour the fishing smack!
Give peace to our pillows,
  Bring our men back!

III. OLD AND NEW TESTAMENT STUDIES

DAVID'S LAMENT OVER SAUL AND JONATHAN

Israel's beauty is slain
  Here on Gilboa's high places,
How are the mighty fallen
  And tears upon all our faces.

Tell it not now in Gath
  Or in Askelon's city name it,
Lest Philistia's daughters rejoice
  And with songs of triumph proclaim it.

Let there be no more dew,
  Gilboa, upon thy mountains!
Over thy fields of offerings fair,
  Holden be all heaven's fountains.

For there the shield of the mighty,
  Even Saul's shield, to-day,
As though he was ne'er the Anointed of God,
  Is vilely cast away.

Till the foe in his blood lay stricken
  Or cloven through and through,
The bow of Jonathan turned not back,
  The sword of Saul still slew.

Lovely were they in their lives,
  In death undivided they lay,
They were swifter than mountain eagles,
  Stronger than lions at bay.

Weep, ye daughters of Israel,
  Weep over Saul your King,
Who clothed you with scarlet and decked you with gold
  And filled you with every good thing.

How are the mighty fallen,
  And all their boasts in vain!
There on Gilboa's high places,
  O Jonathan, thou wast slain.

Alas! my brother Jonathan,
  I am sore distressed for thee;
For thou hast been very pleasant,
  Very pleasant to me.

Beyond the love of woman
  Was the love that for me you bore.
How are the mighty fallen
  And perished the weapons of war!

THE FIERY FURNACE

Bound into the furnace blazing
　They have cast the Children Three;
But oh! miracle amazing,
　They arise, unscathed and free;
While through paths of fire, to guide them,
　Paths no other foot has trod--
Lo! A Fourth is seen beside them,
　Shining like the Son of God.

Ah! not ours their saintly measure,
　Yet 'tis still our heart's desire,
That Thou wouldst of Thy good pleasure,
　Teach us, too, to walk the fire--
Living lives of stern denial,
　Trusty toiler, helpmeet tried,
Till grown fit for fiery trial,
　With our Saviour at our side.

RUTH AND NAOMI

When Judges ruled the tribes of Israel,
A cruel famine on the people fell,
Till even Bethlehem, the "House of Bread,"
For meat and drink at last was sore bestead.

Then when they called upon Jehovah's name,
This answer to their heart's petition came:
"Send forth your strong into the land where Lot
The might of Moab and his race begot--

"Your kinsfolk they: there still the streams run quick,
Still grass and corn are laughing high and thick."
Therefore adventuring forth, the bold and strong
Their famished flocks and herds drove each along,

Till Moab's high-set plain and warm, wide valleys
Wherefrom clear-watered Arnon westward sallies,
Rejoiced they reached: there welcome found and there
Release from want, of wealth a goodly share.

With these Elimelech and his precious ones,
His wife Naomi and his two brave sons,
Mahlon and Chilion, Jordan's shrunken tide
Crossed, and at Hesbon stayed and occupied.

And there they prospered for a blessed time
Until Elimelech in his lordly prime,
Hasting those cattle-spoilers to pursue,
The ambuscading sons of Anak slew.

Then Chilion and Mahlon, by the voice
Of their good mother guided, made their choice
Amongst the maids of Moab for their wives:
And so, a ten years' space lived joyful lives.

Till pestilence o'ertook the brothers; naught
Of wives' or mothers' care availed them aught,
But, blessing both, their sight was quenched in gloom;
Three widows wept o'er their untimely tomb.

Then when their days of mourning now were o'er,
Fresh tidings came from Jordan's further shore:
"Judaea's years of famine now are passed,
And joyous plenty crowns her fields at last."

Naomi then outspake: "Dear daughters lone,
Yea, dearer for their sakes who now are gone
Than if indeed ye were my very own
Born children, hearken to Naomi's voice
Who of all Moabs' maids made you her choice!

"Good wives and fond, as ever cherished
Husband, were ye unto my two sons dead,
Diligent weavers of their household wool,
True joy-mates when their cup of bliss was full,
Kind comforters in sorrow or in pain.
Alloy was none, but one to mar life's golden chain.

"No child, dear Orpah, loving Ruth, have ye
To suckle or to dance upon your knee,
No other sons have I your hearts to woo--
Grandchildren can be none from me to you.
Therefore, my daughters, O, consider well

Since you are young, and fair and so excel
In every homecraft, were it not more wise
No longer to refuse to turn your eyes
Towards the suitors brave who, now your days
Of mourning are accomplished, fix their gaze
Upon your goings? Verily now 'twere right
That you should each a noble Moabite
Espouse, till, with another's love accost,
Your childless grief in motherhood be lost.
And I, why should I tarry longer here
To be a burden on you year by year?
Kinsfolk and friends have I at Bethlehem
Where plenty reigns; I will go back to them--"
Then much they both besought her to remain,
And yet her purpose neither could restrain;
Therefore her goods to gather she began
Against the passing of the caravan.
But Ruth and Orpah each prepared also
Beside her unto Bethlehem to go.

And now the three stand ready, full of tears
To quit the haunts of happy married years,
The tombs that hid their lost ones. Staunchly then
Naomi spoke her purpose once again:
"Daughters, turn back, each to her mother's house
To take the rest that there her work allows,
And in due course a second husband find,
Nor be unto the future foolish--blind!
Yet take a blessing from the heart of hearts
Of your Naomi ere she hence departs."

She blessed them, and with voices lifted up
In loud lament the dregs of sorrow's cup

They drained together. Orpah, weeping, turned
And slowly went, but Ruth with eyes that yearned
Into Naomi's, cried aloud in pain:
"Thus to forsake thee, urge me not again,
Nor to return from following after thee!
For where thou goest, I will surely go.
And where thou lodgest, will I lodge also!
Thy people shall be my people evermore,
And thy God only will I now adore!
And where thou diest, I will buried be!
So may Jehovah strike me with his thunder,
If aught but only death our lives shall sunder."

Ruth's lips have sealed that solemn covenant,
Then with Naomi hand in hand she went.

But as they slept that night there came to each
The selfsame vision, though they ne'er had speech
Thereon, till Obed's birth, Ruth's only son
And David's grandsire; for they each saw one
With Mahlon's aspect seated in the skies,
And on his knees a babe with Ruth's own eyes,
And by the infant's side one with a face
Ruddy and bold, a form of Kingly grace,
And in his hand a harp wherefrom he drew
Marvellous music while his songs thereto
Held hosts of angels hearkening in the blue.
Then figures floated o'er him faint and far
Up to a Child who rode upon a star,
And in the Heavenly wonder of his face,
They read the Ransom of the Human Race.

THE LILIES OF THE FIELD AND THE FOWLS OF THE AIR

"Consider the lilies!" He spake as yet spake no man:
  "Consider the lilies, the lilies of the leas,
They toil not, they spin not, like you, tired man and woman,
  Yet Solomon in his glory was not robed like one of these.

"Consider the lilies! Sure, if your Heavenly Father
  So clothe the meadow grasses that here flower free of scathe
And to-morrow light the oven, now, say, shall he not rather
  Still of His goodness clothe you, O ye of little faith?

"Consider the fowls of the air, behind your harrows;
  They plough not, they reap not, nor gather grain away,
Yet your Heavenly Father cares for them; then, if he feed the sparrows,
  Shall He not rather feed you, His children, day by day?"

THE GOOD PHYSICIAN

To find Him they flock, young and old, from their cities,
  With hearts full of hope: for the tidings had spread:
"The proud He rebukes and the poorest He pities,
  Recovers the leper, upraises the dead."

So the shepherd has left his sheep lone on the mountain,
  The woodman his axe buried fast in the pine,

The maiden her pitcher half-filled at the fountain,
  The housewife her loom and the fisher his line.

With their babes on their bosoms, their sick on their shoulders,
  Toilsomely thronging by footpath and ford,
Now resting their burthens among the rude boulders,
  Still they come climbing in search of the Lord.

Until on the Mount, with the morn they have found Him--
  Christ, the long sought--they have found Him at length,
With their sick and their stricken, in faith they flock round Him,
  As sighing He looks up to Heaven for strength.

He has touched the deaf ears and the blind eyes anointed--
  And straightway they hear Him and straightway they see;
Laid hands on the lame and they leap, supple-jointed,
  The devils denounced and affrighted they flee.

Yea? for their faith, from each life-long affliction,
  Yea, for their faith from their sins they are freed,
And therefore have earned His divine benediction--

                *   *   *   *   *

Stretch forth Thy hand, for as sore is our need.

Lord! we are deaf, we are dumb, lost in blindness,
  Lepers and lame and by demons possessed!
Lord, we are dead! of Thine infinite kindness
  Restore us, redeem! bear us home on Thy breast.

THE SOWER

A Sower went forth to sow,
  But His seed on the wayside showered;
A bird-flock out of the air flashed low
  And the goodly grain devoured.

A Sower went forth to sow,
  O'er hid rocks plying his toil;
The seed leaped up at the warm sun's glow,
  But withered for lack of soil.

A Sower went forth to sow,
  And his seed took steadfast root;
But flaming poppies and thorns in row
  Sprang up and strangled the fruit.

A Sower went forth to sow,
  And at last his joy he found;
For his good seed's generous overflow
  Sank deep into gracious ground.

Lord, when we look back on our lives,
  With penitent sighs and tears,
Our evil that with Thee strives and strives
  In Thy parable's truth appears.

As the wayside hard were our hearts,
  Where Thy good seed lightly lay,
For the Devil's flock, as it downward darts,
  To bruise and to bear away.

Thy winged words falling nigher
  Sprang up in our souls with haste,
But they could not endure temptation's fire
  And withered and went to waste.

Within us Thy word once more
  Thou sowest, but--sore beset
With worldly weeds--for Thy threshing floor
  Shall it ever ripen yet?

Yea, Lord, it shall if Thou please,
  In passionate, patient prayer,
To draw the nation upon its knees
  And fill it with Heavenly care.

And so shall we all arise
  In the joy of a soul's re-birth
To hold a communion with the skies
  That shall bring down Heaven to earth.

THE PRODIGAL'S RETURN

(From the Scotch Gaelic)

Tedious grew the time to me
  Within the Courts of Blessing;
My secure felicity,
  For folly I forswore;

Vain delusion wrought my woe
  Till now, in want distressing,
I go begging to and fro
  Upon an alien shore.

In my dear old home of peace,
  Around my father's table
Many a servant sits at ease
  And eats and drinks his fill;
While within a filthy stall
  With loathsome swine I stable,
Sin-defiled and scorned of all
  To starve on husk and swill.

Ah, how well I mind me
  Of the happy days gone over!
Love was then behind me,
  Before me, and around;
Then, light as air, I leapt,
  A laughing little rover,
Now dull and heavy-stepped
  I pace this desert ground.

Sin with flattering offers came;
  Against my Sire rebelling
I yielded my good name
  At the Tempter's easy smile;
In fields that were not ours,
  Brighter blooming, richer smelling,
I ravished virgin flowers
  With a heart full of guile.

'Twas thus an open shame

In the sight of all the Noble,
Yea! a monster I became,
  Till my gold ceased to flow,
And my fine fair-weather friends
  Turned their backs upon my trouble.
Now an outcast to Earth's ends
  Under misery I go.

Yet though bitter my disgrace,
  Than every ill severer
Is the thought of the face
  Of the Sire for whom I long.
I shall see Him no more
  Though to me he now is dearer
Than he ever was, before
  I wrought him such wrong.

And yet ere I die
  I will journey forth to meet him.
Home I will hie,
  For he yet may be won.
For Pardon and Peace
  My soul will entreat him,
"Father, have grace
  On thy Prodigal Son!"

Could I get near enough
  To send him a message--
I keeping far off--
  He would not say me nay.
In some little nook
  He would find me a living
And let none be driving

His shamed son away.

The Penitent arose,
  His scalding tears blinding him;
Hope's ray lit his way
  As homeward he pressed.
Afar off his father's
  Fond eyes are finding him,
And the old man gathers
  His boy to his breast.

ST. MARY MAGDALEN

They who have loved the most
  The most have been forgiven,
And with the Devil's host
  Most mightily have striven.
And so it was of old
  With her, once all unclean,
Now of the saints white-stoled--
  Mary, the Magdalen.
For though in Satan's power
  She seemed for ever fast,
Her Saviour in one hour
  Seven devils from her cast.

O'erburthened by the weight
  Of her black bosom sin,

As Christ with Simon sate
　At meat, she had stolen in.
Toward her Lord she drew;
　She knelt by Him unchid;
The latchet of His shoe
　Her trembling hands undid.
Foot-water none was by
　Nor towel, as was meet,
To comfort and to dry
　His hot way-weary feet;
But with her blinding tears
　She bathes them now instead,
And dries them with the hairs
　Of her abased head.

And so, when Simon looked,
　And pondered, evil-eyed,
No longer Jesus brooked
　His thought, but thus replied;
"Simon, no kiss of peace
　Thou gav'st me at thy door,
No oil, my head to ease,
　Didst thou upon it pour,
Nay, for thy bidden guest
　So little hast thou cared,
His weary feet to rest
　No bath hadst thou prepared;
Yet hath this woman here,
　By thee with scorn decried,
Washed them with many a tear,
　And with her tresses dried,
And given them, from her store
　Of spikenard, cool relief,

And kissed them o'er and o'er
  In penitential grief.
Therefore her joy begins,
  Her prayer is heard in heaven;
Though many are her sins,
  They all shall be forgiven!"
Scant mercy he receives
  Whose love for God is small;
But he whom God forgives
  The most, loves most of all.

IV. CHURCH FESTIVALS

A CHRISTMAS COMMUNION HYMN

(After the Meditation for Communion on Christmas Day in *Eucharistica*)

Welcome, thrice blessed day! thrice blessed hour!
  To hail you, every heart to Heaven is climbing,
The while the snow in softly circling shower
  Draws down to meet them 'mid the joybell's chiming;
Like blessed morsels of that manna bread
Wherewith of old the Lord His People fed.

Welcome, dear dawn! if now no Angel Song
  With sudden ravishing acclaim salute thee,
Yet everywhere Our Church's white-robed throng
  Shall to thy first exultancy transmute thee.
Peace and Good Will again with holy mirth
Proclaiming to the Universal Earth.

Then, too, my soul, forth summoning all thy powers,
  Thyself from worldly schemes and wishes sunder,
To worship and admire this hour of hours
  That is all miracle and the height of wonder;

Infinity itself shrinks to a span,
Since God, remaining God, becometh Man.

Here is a mother with no mortal mate!
  Here is a son that hath no earthly father!
A graft, on Adam's stock incorporate,
  Who yet therefrom no mortal taint can gather!
A Babe to whom a new and glorious Star
Earth's Wisest Kings for worship draws from far.

All hail! then, sweetest Saviour, thrice all hail!
  The King of Kings, by David's prophesying;
Yet on no royal couch Thy first weak wail
  Awoke, for in a manger Thou wast lying:
Still for that condescension more a King
Than having all the whole world's wealth could bring.

Thus with Earth's humblest brothering thy estate,
  Thus to Earth's mightiest giving meek example,
The lowly Thou exaltest to be great,
  The proud thou teachest on their pride to trample.
So, turning poor men rich and rich men poor,
For each Thou makest his salvation sure.

A CHRISTMAS CAROL OF THE EPIPHANY

Now who are these who from afar
Follow yon solitary star?

Whence journey they and what the quest
That turns their faces towards the west?

Three Kings are they and Mages three,
Who in their camel company,
With offerings rich, still onward press,
Across the wintry wilderness.

Nine months agone, Isaiah's page
They pondered o'er with questioning sage,
When underneath their wondering eyes
His words were altered in this wise:

"Behold a Virgin hath conceived!"
They saw, and marvelled, and believed,
And hasted forth upon the morn
To greet the King that should be born.

Afar they fared by land and flood,
The while they saw, with bounding blood,
A star that did all stars exceed
In wonder still their footsteps lead.

Until, amid the falling snow,
They found the Highest laid most low;
His palace but a cattle shed,
A manger for His princely bed.

And there they bent with holy joy
And hope before the new-born Boy;
And opened, at His infant feet,
Their royal offerings rich and sweet.

A FOURTEENTH-CENTURY CAROL

When God came down on Earth to dwell,
    Great cold befell:
Yet Mary on the road hath seen
    A fig-tree green.
Said Joseph: "O Mary, let the fruit hang;
For thirty good mile we have still to gang,
    Lest we be late!"

When Mary unto a village door
    At last did win,
She thus bespake the cottager:
    "Sir, take us in!
Since for this young Child's tender sake
A pitying heart must surely ache,
    The night's so cold."

"You're welcome all to my ox-stall!"
    The good man cried.
But in the middle of the night
    He rose and sighed:
"Where are ye now, poor hapless ones?
That ye're not frozen to the bones,
    I marvel much."

Then back into his house he runs
    From forth the byre--
"Rouse up, rouse up, my dearest wife,
    And light a fire,
As fine as ever sent up smoke,

Whereat these poor and perishing folk
  May comfort them."

Mary with joy into the house
  The Babe has brought,
Joseph her just and faithful spouse,
  His wallet sought.
Therefrom he took a kettle small;
Some snow the Child therein let fall,
  And lo 'tis flour!

Thereto the Babe has added ice;
  'Tis sugar straight!
Now water drops, and, in a trice,
  'Tis milk most sweet!
The kettle, fast as you could look,
They hung upon the kitchen hook
  A meal to cook.

The godly Joseph carved a spoon
  From out a brand;
To ivory it changed full soon
  And adamant.
When Mary gave the Babe the food,
He became Jesus, Son of God.
  Before their eyes.

EARTH'S EASTER

She the long sought for and sighed for in vain, the enchantress immortal--
Spring, in our very despair, out of inviolate air
Charioting summons the Eastern gate; the obedient portal
Opes, and a vision blest yields to the wondering West.

High on her crystal car she trembles in halycon tissues,
Gently with golden curb checking her coursers superb--
All her ethereal beauty elate with Love's infinite issues,
Whilst this enchantment slips forth from her sibylline lips:
"Herb and tree in your kinds, free lives of the mountain and forest,
Shoals of the stream and the flood, flights of the welkin and wood,
Herd and flock of the field, and ye, whose need is the sorest,
Suffering spirits of men, lo! I am with you again.
Fear no more for the tyrant hoar as he rushes to battle
Armoured in ice, and darts lance after lance at your hearts,
Fear not his flaming bolts as they hurtle with horrible rattle
Out of the lurid inane fulminant over the plain.
Fear not his wizardry white that circles and circles and settles
Stealthily hour by hour, feathery flower upon flower,
Over the spell-bound sleeper, till last the pitiless petals
Darkly in icy death stifle his labouring breath.

"Late upon yon white height the despot his fugitives rallied,
Deeming the crest snow-crowned still inaccessibly frowned;
Idly, for instant upon him my bright-speared chivalry sallied,
Smote and far into the North swept him discomfited forth,
Therefore, from root unto hole, from hole into burgeoning branches,
Tendril and tassel and cup now let the ichor leap up:
Therefore, with flowering drift and with fluttering bloom avalanches,

Snowdrop and silver thorn laugh baffled winter to scorn;
Primrose, daffodil, cowslip, shine back to my shimmering sandals,
Hyacinth host, o'er the green flash your cerulean sheen,
Lilac, your perfumed lamps, light, chestnut, your clustering candles,
Broom and laburnum, untold torches of tremulous gold!
Therefore gold-gather again from the honeyed heath and the bean field,
Snatching no instant of ease, bright, multitudinous bees!
Therefore, ye butterflies, float and flicker from garden to green field,
Flicker and float and stay, settle and sip and away!

"Therefore race it and chase it, ye colts, in the emerald meadow!
Round your serious dams frisk, ye fantastical lambs!
Therefore, bird unto bird, from the woodland's wavering shadow
Pipe and 'plain and protest, flutter together and nest.

"Therefore, ye skylarks, in shivering circle still higher and higher
Soar, and the palpitant blue drench with delirious dew.
Therefore, nightingale, lost in the leaves, or lone on the brier,
Under the magic moon lift your tumultuous tune.
Therefore refresh you, faint hearts, take comfort, ye souls sorrow-stricken,
Winning from nature relief, courage and counsel in grief,
Judging that He, whose handmaid I am, out of death to requicken
Year after year His earth into more exquisite birth,
Shadows thereby to your souls through what drear and perilous places
Into what Paradise blest beacons His searching behest--
Even the Heaven of Heavens where fond, long-hungered-for faces
Into your own shall shine radiant with rapture divine."

EASTER DAY, 1915

I

The stars die out on Avon's watchful breast,
  While simple shepherds climb through shadows grey,
With beating bosoms up the Wrekin's Crest
  To see the sun "dance in" an Easter Day
Whose dawning consummates three centuries--
  Since Shakespeare's death and entrance to the skies--
Resolved the radiant miracle not to miss
  Reserved alone to earliest opened eyes.
We, too, with faces set towards the East,
  Our joyful orison offerings yielding up
Keep with our risen Lord His Pascal feast
  From Paten Blest and Consecrated Cup,
And give Him thanks Who of all realms of Earth
Made England richest by her Shakespeare's birth.

II

"St. George for Merrie England!" let us cry
  And each a red rose pin upon his breast,
Then face the foe with fearless front and eye
  Through all our frowning leaguer in the West.
For not alone his Patron Day it is
  Wherefrom our noble George hath drawn his name;
Three centuries and a half gone by ere this;
  By Shakespeare's birth it won a second fame.
A greater glory is its crown to-day

Since at its first and faintest uttered breath
A mighty angel rolled the stone away
  That sealed His tomb Who captive now leads death,
And thereby did the great example give.
That they who die for others most shall live.

THE ASCENSION

When Christ their Lord, to Heaven upraised,
  Was wafted from the Apostles' sight,
And upwards wistfully they gazed
  Into the far, blue Infinite,
Behold two men in white apparel dressed
Who thus bespake them on the mountain crest:

"Why stand ye, men of Galilee,
  So sadly gazing on the skies?
For this same Jesus, whom ye see
  Caught in the clouds to Paradise,
Shall in like manner from the starry height
Return again to greet your joyful sight."

Would, O Lord Jesus! thus to hear
  Thy farewell words we too had met,
Among Thine own Disciples dear,
  Upon the brow of Olivet!
Yet are we blest, though of that joy bereaved,
Who having seen Thee not, have yet believed.

O, then in each succeeding year
  When Thine Ascension Day draws round,
With hearts so full of holy fear
  May we within Thy Church be found,
That in the spirit we may see Thee rise
And bless us with pierced hands from out the skies!

Christ, if our gaze for ever thus
  Is fixed upon Thy Heavenward way,
Death shall but bring to each of us
  At last his soul's Ascension Day,
Till in Thy mercy Thou descend once more
And quick and dead to meet Thy coming soar.

WHITSUNTIDE

When Christ from off the mountain crest
  Before their marvelling eyes,
Whilst His disciples still He blessed,
  Was caught into the skies--
The Angels, whose harmonious breath
  Erstwhile proclaimed His birth,
Now hailed Him Victor over Death,
  Redeemer of the Earth;
"Lift up your heads, ye Heavenly Gates!"
  Rang forth their joyful strain;
"For lo! the King of Glory waits
  To enter you again!"

Thus, heralded, from Heaven to Heaven
  Magnifical He goes,
Until the last of all the seven
  To greet His coming glows;
While He the Eternal long left lone
  To meet Him doth upstand,
Then sets His Son upon the Throne
  Once more at His right hand.
Whereat with one triumphal hymn
  Majestically blent
The Cherubim and Seraphim
  The Universe have rent.
Last, from the splendrous mercy seat,
  Of Father and of Son,
To Earth, their purpose to complete,
  Descends the Promised One.

Like to a mighty rushing wind
  He falls, subduing space,
To where Christ's chosen with one mind
  Are gathered in one place.
With tongues of flame He lights on each,
  Whose wonder-working spell
Fires them in every human speech
  Heaven's message forth to tell.
The coward brood of doubt and fear
  And hesitance are fled;
Before the quickening Comforter
  They rise as from the dead.
The bolted door is yawning wide,
  The barred gate backward flung;
And forth unarmed and fearless-eyed,
  They fare their foes among.

HARVEST HYMN

CAST THY BREAD UPON THE WATERS

O ye weeping sons and daughters,
  Trust the Heavenly Harvest Giver,
Cast your bread upon the waters
  Of His overflowing river;
Cast the good seed, nothing doubting
  That your tears shall turn to praise,
Ye shall yet behold it sprouting
  Heavenward, after many days.

Hope and love, long frost-withholden,
  Into laughing life upleaping,
Blade and ear, from green to golden,
  Yet shall ripen for your reaping;
Till some radiant summer morrow,
  Wheresoe'er your sickle cleaves,
Ye, who sow to-day in sorrow,
  Shout for joy amid your sheaves.

O then, learn the inmost meaning
  Of your harvest's rich redundance,
Bid the famished ones come gleaning
  In the fields of your abundance;
So in overrunning measure
  Shall your thankful fellow-men
Give you, of their hearts' hid treasure,

All your good gifts back again.

Till, ye faithful sons and daughters,
  God your golden lives deliver,
Like the good grain to the waters
  Of death's overflowing river;
Till up-caught amid His sleepers,
  Heavenly fruit from earthly loam,
At the last, His angel reapers
  On their bosoms bear you home.

V. GOOD AND FAITHFUL SERVANTS

FATHER O'FLYNN

Of priests we can offer a charming variety,
Far renowned for larning and piety;
Still, I'd advance you, widout impropriety,
    Father O'Flynn as the flower of them all.

Chorus: Here's a health to you, Father O'Flynn,
            Slainte and slainte, and slainte agin;
                Powerfullest preacher, and
                Tenderest teacher, and
            Kindliest creature in ould Donegal.

Don't talk of your Provost and Fellows of Trinity,
Famous for ever for Greek and Latinity,
Dad, and the divels and all at Divinity,
    Father O'Flynn 'd make hares of them all.
        Come, I vinture to give you my word,
        Never the likes of his logic was heard.
            Down from Mythology
            Into Thayology,
    Troth! and Conchology, if he'd the call.

Chorus: Here's a health to you, etc.

Och! Father O'Flynn, you've the wonderful way wid you,
All the ould sinners are wishful to pray wid you,
All the young childer are wild for to play wid you,
   You've such a way wid you, Father avick!
     Still, for all you've so gentle a soul,
     Gad, you've your flock in the grandest conthroul
       Checkin' the crazy ones,
       Coaxin' onaisy ones,
   Liftin' the lazy ones on wid the stick.
   Chorus: Here's a health to you, etc.

And though quite avoidin' all foolish frivolity,
Still at all saisons of innocent jollity,
Where was the play-boy could claim an equality
   At comicality, Father, wid you?
    Once the Bishop looked grave at your jest,
    Till this remark set him off wid the rest:
     "Is it lave gaiety
     All to the laity?
   Cannot the clargy be Irishmen too?"
   Chorus: Here's a health to you, etc.

LADY GWENNY

County by county for beauty and bounty
  Go search! and this pound to a penny,
When you've one woman to show us as human
  And lovely as our Lady Gwenny;
For she has the scorn for all scorners,
And she has the tear for all mourners,
  Yet joying with joy,
  With no crabb'd annoy
To pull down her mouth at the corners.

Up with the lark in the pasture you'll meet with her,
  Songs like his own sweetly trilling,
Carrying now for some poor folk a treat with her,
  Small mouths with lollypops filling:
And while, as he stands in a puzzle,
She strokes the fierce bull on his muzzle,
  The calves and the lambs
  Run deserting their dams
In her kind hands their noses to nuzzle.

Now with her maidens a sweet Cymric cadence
  She leads, just to lighten their sewing;
Now at the farm, her food basket on arm,
  She has set all the cock'rels a-crowing.
The turkey-cock strutting and strumming,
His bagpipe puts by at her humming,
  And even the old gander,
  The fowl-yard's commander,
He winks his sly eye at her coming.

Never to wandering minstrel or pondering
　Poet her castle gate closes:
Ever her kindly cheer--ever her praise sincere
　Falls like the dew on faint roses.
And when her Pennillions rhyming
She mates to her triple harp's chiming,
　In her green Gorsedd gown--
　The half of the town
Up the fences to hear her are climbing.

Men in all fashions have pleaded their passions--
　The scholar, the saint, and the sinner,
Pleaded in vain Lady Gwenny to gain,--
　For only a hero shall win her:
And to share his strong work and sweet leisure
He'll have no keen chaser of pleasure,
　But a loving young beauty
　With a soul set on duty,
And a heart full of heaven's hid treasure.

OLD DOCTOR MACK

Ye may tramp the world over from Delhi to Dover,
  And sail the salt say from Archangel to Arragon;
Circumvint back through the whole Zodiack,
But to ould Docther Mack ye can't furnish a paragon.
Have ye the dropsy, the gout, the autopsy?
  Fresh livers and limbs instantaneous he'll shape yez;
No way infarior in skill, but suparior
  And lineal postarior to ould Aysculapius.

Chorus: He and his wig wid the curls so carroty,
             Aigle eye and complexion clarety;
                Here's to his health,
                Honour and wealth,
             The king of his kind and the cream of all charity.

How the rich and the poor, to consult for a cure,
Crowd on to his door in their carts and their carriages,
Showin' their tongues or unlacin' their lungs,
For divel wan sympton the docther disparages,
Troth an' he'll tumble for high or for humble
  From his warm feather-bed wid no cross contrariety;
Makin' as light of nursin' all night
  The beggar in rags as the belle of society.

Chorus: He and his wig wid the curls, etc.

And, as if by a meracle, ailments hysterical,
  Dad, wid one dose of bread pills he can smother,
And quench the love sickness wid comical quickness,

Prescribin' the right boys and girls to each other.
And the sufferin' childer! Your eyes 'twould bewilder,
  To see the wee craythurs his coat-tails unravellin'--
Each of them fast on some treasure at last,
  Well knowin' ould Mack's just a toy-shop out travellin'.

Chorus: He and his wig wid the curls, etc.

Thin, his doctherin' done, in a rollickin' run
  Wid the rod or the gun he's the foremost to figure;
Be Jupiter Ammon! what jack-snipe or salmon
  E'er rose to backgammon his tail-fly or trigger!
And hark that view-holloa! 'Tis Mack in full follow
  On black "Faugh-a-ballagh" the country-side sailin'!
Och, but you'd think 'twas ould Nimrod in pink,
  Wid his spurs cryin' chink over park wall and palin'.

Chorus: He and his wig wid the curls so carroty,
        Aigle eye and complexion clarety.
           Here's to his health,
           Honour and wealth,
        Hip, hip, hooray, wid all hilarity!

        Hip, hip, hooray! That's the way!
         All at once widout disparity!
        One more cheer for our docther dear,
        The king of his kind and the cream of all charity,
           Hip, hip, hooray!

TO THE MEMORY OF JOHN OWEN

HARLECH CHOIRMASTER

Who is this they bear along the street
In his coffin through the sunshine sweet?
Who is this so many comrades crave,
Turn by turn, to carry to the grave?

Who is this for whom the hillward track
Glooms with mounting lines of mourners black?
Till the Baptists' green old burial-ground
Clasps them all within its quiet bound.

Here John Owen we must lay to rest,
'Tis for him our hearts are sore distressed;
Since his sister wistfully he eyed,
Bowed his head upon her breast and died.

Well and truly at his work he wrought;
Every Harlech road to order brought;
Then through winter evenings dark and long
At the chapel gave his heart to song.

Till before his gesture of command--
Till before his hushing voice and hand--
Sweeter, fuller strains who could desire
Than he charmed from out his Baptist choir.

Many a time the passer-by enchained
By their rapture to its close remained,

And the churches joyfully agreed
Their united choirs his skill should lead.

So in Handel's choruses sublime
He would train them for the Christmas time;
Mould their measures for the concert hall,
Roll their thunders round the Castle wall.

Loving husband, tender father, quick
To console the suffering and sick--
Christ to follow was his constant aim,
Christ's own deacon ere he bore the name.

Widowed wife and children fatherless,
Stricken kinsfolk, friends in keen distress--
Sorrow swept them all beneath its wave
As his coffin sank into the grave.

But his Pastor's fervent voice went forth,
Delicately dwelling on his worth,
Urging his example, till at last
Heavenly comfort o'er our grief he cast.

For his lonely ones we bowed in prayer,
Sighed one hymn, and left him lying there,
Whispering: "Lord, Thy will be done to-day,
Thou didst give him, Thou hast taken away."

SAINT CUTHBERT

When once a winter storm upon the shores of Fife
  Drave Cuthbert; in despair, one fearful comrade saith:
"To land in such a storm is certain loss of life!"
  "Return," another cried, "by sea is equal death."
Then Cuthbert, "Earth and sea against us both are set,
But friends, look up, for Heaven lies open to us yet."

ALFRED THE GREAT

A MILLENARY MEMORIAL

"In my life I have striven to live so worthily that at my death I may
leave but a memory of good works to those who come after me."

Thus Alfred spake, whose days were beads of prayer
  Upon the rosary of his royal time,
Who let "I do" wait not upon "I dare,"
  Yet both with duty kept in golden chime,
Who, great in victory, greater in defeat,
  Greatest in strenuous peace, still suffering, planned
From Ashdown's field to Athelney's lone retreat
  Upward for aye to lift his little land.
Therefore the seed of his most fruitful sowing,
  A thousand years gone by, on earth and sea,

From slender strength to stately empire growing
   Hath given our isle great continents in fee.
For which on Alfred's death-day each true heart
   Goes out in praise of his immortal part.

SIR SAMUEL FERGUSON

Strong Son of Fergus, with thy latest breath
   Thou hast lent a joy unto the funeral knell,
   Welcoming with thy whispered "All is well!"
The awful aspect of the Angel Death.
As, strong in life, thou couldst not brook to shun
   The heat and burthen of the fiery day,
   Fronting defeat with stalwart undismay,
And wearing meekly honours stoutly won.
Pure lips, pure hands, pure heart were thine, as aye
   Erin demanded from her bards of old,
   And, therefore, on thy harpstrings of pure gold
Has waked once more her high heroic lay.
   What shoulders now shall match the mighty fold
Of Ossian's mantle? Thou hast passed away.

"MEN, NOT WALLS, MAKE A CITY"

(On the home-coming of the London Regiments after the Boer War)

London Town, hear a ditty,
  While we crown our comrades true:
"Men, not walls, make a City;"
  Ill befalls when men are few,--

Ill indeed when from his duty
  Into greed the burgess falls,
Every hand on bribe and booty--
  How shall stand that City's walls?

Never yet upon thine annals
  Hath been writ such a shame;
Never down such crooked channels,
  London Town, thy commerce came.

On the poor no tyrant burden,
  Debt secure and sacred trust,
Honest gain and generous guerdon,
  These remain thy record just.

Therefore still through all thy story
  Loyal will thy train-bands led
Forth to feats of patriot glory,
  Back through streets with bays o'erspread.

Therefore when the trumpet's warning
  Out again for battle rang,

As of old all peril scorning,
  Forth thy bold young burghers sprang;

Faced the fight, endured the prison,
  Through the night of doubt and gloom,
Till the Empire's star new risen
  Chased afar the clouds of doom.

Therefore, when their ranks came marching,
  Home again with flashing feet,
Under bays of triumph arching
  City ways and City Street;

London, lift to God thanksgiving
  For His Gift that passes all--
For thy heroes, dead and living,
  Who have made thy City Wall.

FIELD-MARSHAL EARL KITCHENER

(June 13, 1916)

A sheet of foam is our great Soldier's shroud
  Beside the desolate Orkney's groaning caves;
And we are desolate and groan aloud
  To know his body wandering with the waves
Who when the thunder-cloud of battle hate
  Broke o'er us, through it towered, the while he bore

Upon his Titan shoulders a world weight
  Of doubt and danger none had brooked before.
For while incredulous friend and foe denied him
  Such possible prowess, Honour's blast he blew;
And lo! as if from out the earth beside him,
  Army on army into order grew;
Till need at last was none for our retreating,
  And back to Belgium and the front of France
We bore, firm gathered for our foe's defeating
  Against the sounding of the Great Advance.

Few were his friends, yet closely round him clustered,
  But from five million Britons, who at his call
Came uncompelled and round him sternly mustered,
  The sighs escape, the silent teardrops fall.

And not alone the Motherland is weeping
  Her great dead Captain but, The Seven Seas o'er,
Daughter Dominions sorrow's watch are keeping,
  For he was theirs as her's in peace and war.

Yea, strong sage Botha, and that stern Cape Raider
  Whom first he fought then bound with friendship's bond--
Each now our own victorious Empire aider--
  Lament his loss the sounding deeps beyond.
And India mourns her mightiest Soldier Warden,
  Egypt the Sirdar who her desert through

Laid iron lines of vengeance for our Gordon
  Till on the Madhi he swept, and struck and slew.
And France, for whom he fought a youthful gallant,
  From whose proud breast he drew Fashoda's thorn--
France who with England shared his searching talent,

France like his second mother stands forlorn.

*   *   *   *   *

A man of men was he, the steadfast glances
  Of whose steel-grey, indomitable eyes
So pierced the mind, behind all countenances,
  Crushed were the sophist's arts, the coward's lies.
A man of men but in his greatness lonely--
  Undaunted in defeat, in conquest calm,
For God and Country living and dying only,
  And winner therefore of the deathless palm.

*   *   *   *   *

A truce to tears then. Though his body hath
  No rest in English earth, his shining soul
Still leads his armies up the arduous path
  He paved for them forthright to Glory's goal.

And we the men and women who remain,
  Let us to be his other Army burn
With such pure fires of sacrificial pain
  As shall reward our warriors' return.

But now a sudden heavy silence falls
  On all our streets, half-mast the standard hangs--
The hearseless funeral passes to St. Paul's,
  And out of every steeple the death-bell clangs.

Now sorrowing King and Queen, as midday booms,
  The hushed Fane enter, while o'er mourners black,

Grey soldier, choral white, quick gleams and glooms
  Of sun and shadow darkle and sparkle back.
The prayers of priest and people to heaven's gate win
  And a choir as of angels welcoming thither our chief--
Till a thunder of drums the mighty Dead March beats in
  And the Last Post lingers, lingers and dies on our grief.

INSCRIPTION FOR A ROLL OF HONOUR IN A PUBLIC SCHOOL

Since to die nobly is Life's act supreme,
  And since our best and dearest thus have died,
Across our cloud of grief a solemn gleam
  Of joy has struck, and all our tears are dried.

For these men to keep pure their country's fame
  Against great odds fell fighting to the death,
God give us grace who here bear on their name
  To grow more like them with each proud-drawn breath.

AN EPITAPH

On an Irish Cross in memory of Charles Graves, Bishop of Limerick

To God his steadfast soul, his starry mind
To Science, a gracious heart to kin and kind,
He living gave. Therefore let each fair bloom
Of Faith and Hope breathe balsam o'er his tomb.

AN INTERCESSIONAL ANSWERED

(June 26, 1902)

We thought to speed our earthly King
 Triumphant on his way
Unto his solemn Sacreing
 Before Thy throne to-day;
His royal robes were wrought, prepared
 His sceptre, orb and crown,
And all earth's Princes here repaired
 To heighten his renown;
When, hurtling out of bluest Heaven,
 Thy bolt upon us fell;
Our head is pierced, our heart is riven,
 Struck dumb the Minster bell.
Yet flags still flutter far and wide;

The league-long garlands glow,
Still London wears her gala pride
  Above a breast of woe.
Lord shall these laughing leaves and flowers
  Their joyful use forget?
Nay, on this stricken realm of ours
  Have Thou compassion yet.

Long years ago our Edward lay
  Thus fighting for his breath,
Yet to such prayers as now we pray
  Thou gavest him back from death.
Then o'er the tempest of his pain,
  His cry of perishing thrill,
Let Thy right arm go forth again,
  Thy saving "Peace! be still!"
Until to all his strength restored
  Thy Spirit lead Him down,
In solemn state, Almighty Lord,
  To take from Thee his crown.

VI. PERSONAL AND VARIOUS

LET THERE BE JOY!

(A Christmas carol from the Scotch Gaelic)

This is now the blessed morn,
  When was born the Virgin's Son,
Who from heights of glorious worth,
  Unto earth His way has won;
All the heav'ns grow bright to greet Him,
Forth to meet Him, ev'ry one!

  All hail! let there be joy!
  All hail! let there be joy!

Mountains praise, with purple splendour,
  Plains, with tender tints, the morn;
Shout, ye waves, with prophesying
  Voices crying, "Christ is born!
Christ, the Son of heav'n's High King,
Therefore sing no more forlorn!"

  All hail! let there be joy!
  All hail! let there be joy!

A HOLIDAY HYMN

He, unto whom the Heavenly Father
  Hath in His works Himself revealed,
Sees with rapt eyes the glory gather
  O'er hill and forest, flood and field.

He, when the torrent laughs in thunder,
  Larks soar exulting in the blue,
Thrills with the waterfall's glad wonder,
  Far up to heaven goes singing too;

Wanders, a child among the daisies;
  Ponders, a poet, all things fair;
Wreathes with the rose of dawn his praises,
  Weaves with eve's passion-flowers his prayer;

Full sure that He who reared the mountain,
  Made smooth the valley, plumed the height,
Holds in clear air the lark and fountain--
  Shall yet uplift him into light.

SUMMER MORNING'S WALK

'Tis scarcely four by the village clock,
  The dew is heavy, the air is cool--
  A mist goes up from the glassy pool,
Through the dim field ranges a phantom flock:
  No sound is heard but the magpie's mock.

Very low is the sun in the sky,
  It needeth no eagle now to regard him.
  Is there not one lark left to reward him
With the shivering joy of his long, sweet cry,
For sad he seemeth, I know not why.

Through the ivied ruins of yonder elm
  There glides and gazes a sadder face;
  Spectre Queen of a vanished race--
'Tis the full moon shrunk to a fleeting film,
And she lingers for love of her ancient realm.

These are but selfish fancies, I know,
  Framed to solace a secret grief--
  Look again--scorning such false relief--
Dwarf not Nature to match thy woe--
Look again! whence do these fancies flow?

What is the moon but a lamp of fire
  That God shall relume in His season? the Sun,
  Like a giant, rejoices his race to run
With flaming feet that never tire
On the azure path of the starry choir.

The lark has sung ere I left my bed:
  And hark! far aloft from those ladders of light
  Many songs, not one only, the morn delight.
Then, sad heart, dream not that Nature is dead,
But seek from her strength and comfort instead.

SNOW-STAINS

The snow had fallen and fallen from heaven,
  Unnoticed in the night,
As o'er the sleeping sons of God
  Floated the manna white;
And still, though small flowers crystalline
  Blanched all the earth beneath,
Angels with busy hands above
  Renewed the airy wreath;
When, white amid the falling flakes,
  And fairer far than they,
Beside her wintry casement hoar
  A dying woman lay.
"More pure than yonder virgin snow
  From God comes gently down,
I left my happy country home,"
  She sighed, "to seek the town,
More foul than yonder drift shall turn,
  Before the sun is high,
Downtrodden and defiled of men,
  More foul," she wept, "am I."

"Yet, as in midday might confessed,
  Thy good sun's face of fire
Draws the chaste spirit of the snow
  To meet him from the mire,
Lord, from this leprous life in death
  Lift me, Thy Magdalene,
That rapt into Redeeming Light
  I may once more be clean."

REMEMBRANCE

(To music)

The fairest blooming flower
  Before the sun must fade;
Each leaf that lights the bower
  Must fall at last decayed!
Like these we too must wither,
  Like these in earth lie low,
None answering whence or whither
  We come, alas! or go.

None answering thee? thou sayest,
  Nay, mourner, from thy heart,
If but in faith thou prayest,
  The Voice Divine shall start;
"I gave and I have taken,
  If thou wouldst comfort win

To cheer thy life forsaken,
  I knock, O, let me in!

"Thy loved ones have but folden
  Their earthly garments by,
And through Heaven's gateway golden
  Gone gladly up on high.
O, if thou wouldst be worthy
  To share their joy anon,
Cast off, cast off the earthy,
  And put the heavenly on!"

SANDS OF GOLD

Hope gave into my trembling hands
An hour-glass running golden sands,
And Love's immortal joys and pains
I measured by its glancing grains.
But Evil Fortune swooped, alas!
Remorseless on the magic glass,
And shivered into idle dust
The radiant record of my trust.

Long I mated with Despair
And craved for Death with ceaseless prayer;
Till unto my sick-bed side
There stole a Presence angel-eyed.

"If thou wouldst heal thee of thy wound,"
Her voice to heavenly harps attuned
Bespake me, "Let the sovran tide
Within this glass thy future guide."
Therewith she gave into my hands
No hour-glass running golden sands,
Only a horologe forlorn
Set against a cross of thorn,
And cold and stern the current seemed
That through its clouded crystal gleamed.

"Immortal one," I cried, "make plain
This cure of my consuming pain.
Open my eyes to understand,
And sift the secrets of this sand,
And measure by its joyless grains
What yet of life to me remains."

"The sand," she said, "that glimmers grey
Within this glass, but yesterday
Was dust at Dives' bolted door
Shaken by God's suffering poor;
Then by blasts of heaven upblown
Before the Judge upon His throne
To swell the ever-gathering cloud
Of witnesses against the proud--
The dust of throats that knew no slaking,
The dust of brows for ever aching--
Dust unto dust with life's last breath
Sighed into the urn of Death."

With tears I took that cross of thorn,
With tears that horologe forlorn.

And all my moments by its dust
I measure now with prayerful trust,
And though my courage oft turns weak,
Fresh comfort from that cross I seek;
In wistful hope I yet may wake
To find the thorn in blossom break,
And from life's shivered glass behold
My being's sands ebb forth in gold.

THE MOURNER

When tears, when heavy tears of sharpest sorrow
  Bathe the lone pillow of the mourner's bed,
Whose grief breaks fresh with every breaking morrow
  For his beloved one dead,
If all be not in vain, his passionate prayer
  Shall like a vapour mount the inviolate blue,
To fall transfigured back on his despair
  In drops of Heavenly dew;

Nor fail him ever but a cloud unceasing
  Of incense from his soul's hushed altar start,
And still return to rise with rich increasing,
  A well-spring from his heart;
Pure fount of peace that freshly overflowing
  Through other lives shall still run radiant on,
Till they, too, reap in joy who wept in sowing,
  Long after he is gone.

DE PROFUNDIS

Out of the darkness I call;
  I stretch forth my hands unto Thee.
Loose these fetters that foully enthral;
  To their lock Thou alone hast the key.
Low at Thy footstool I fall,
  Forgive and Thy servant is free!

Folly took hold of my time,
  On pleasure I perched, to my woe;
I was snared in The Evil One's lime
  And now all his promptings I know.
Crimson as blood is my crime.
  Yet Thou canst wash whiter than snow.

Heaven overhead is one frown;
  About me the black waters rave;
To the deep I go dreadfully down;
  O pluck my feet out of the grave;
Lord! I am sinking, I drown,
  O save, for Thou only canst save.

IMMORTAL HOPE

Summer hath too short a date
 Autumn enters, ah! how soon,
Scattering with scornful hate
 All the flowers of June.
Nay say not so,
Nothing here below
  But dies
  To rise
Anew with rarer glow.

Now, no skylarks singing soar
 Sunward, now, beneath the moon
Love's own nightingale no more
 Lifts her magic tune!
Nay, say not so,
But awhile they go;
  Their strain
  Again
All heaven shall overflow.

WE HAD A CHILD

We had a child, a little Fairy Prince,
  Let loose from Elfland for our heart's delight;
Ah! was it yesterday or four years since
  He beamed upon our sight?
Four years--and yet it seems but yesterday
  Since the blue wonder of his baby eyes.
Beneath their ebon-fringed canopies,
  Subdued us to his sway.

Three years--and yet but yestermorn it seems
  Since first upon his feet he swaying stood,
Buoyed bravely up by memory's magic dreams
  Of elfin hardihood.
He stood, the while that long-forgotten lore
  Lit all his lovely face with frolic glee;
  And then--O marvel! to his mother's knee
Walked the wide nursery floor.

Two years gone by--ah, no! but yesterday
  Our bright-eyed nursling, swift as we could teach,
Forsook the low soft croonings of the fay
  For broken human speech--
Broken, yet to our ears divinelier broken
  Than sweetest snatches from Heaven's mounting bird--
  More eloquent than the poet's passionate word
Supremely sung or spoken.

But O, our darling in his joyful dance
  Tottered death-pale beneath the withering north,

Into a kinder clime, most blessed chance,
  We caught him swiftly forth,
And there he bloomed again, our fairy boy,
  Two year-long Aprils through in sun and shower,
  Wing-footed Mercury of each merry hour,
The Genius of our joy.

And evermore we shared his shifting mood
  Of hide-and-seek with April joy and sorrow,
Till not one shadow of solicitude
  Remained to mar our morrow;
Yea, every fear had flown, lest, welladay!
  The headlong heats or winter's piercing power
  Should light afresh upon our radiant flower
And wither him away.

             *   *   *   *   *

We had a child, a little fairy child,
  He kissed us on the lips but yesternight,
Yet when he wakened his blue eyes were wild
  With fevered light.
We had a child--what countless ages since,
  Did he go forth from us with wildered brain,
  Will he come back and kiss us once again--
Our little Fairy Prince?

BY THE BEDSIDE OF A SICK CHILD

O Thou by whose eternal plan
  Ages arise and roll,
Who in Thine image madest man
  To search him to the soul,
If e'er in token of the Cross,
  With infant arms outspread,
Thou sawest Thy Beloved toss
  In anguish on His bed;
Or heardest in the childish cry
  That pierced the cottage room
The voice of Christ in agony
  Breaking from Calvary's gloom,
Give ear! and from Thy Throne above
  With eyes of mercy mild,
Look down, of Thine immortal love,
  Upon our suffering child.

Though Earth's physicians all in vain
  Have urged their utmost skill,
Yet to our prayers O make it plain
  That Thou canst succour still;
Yea! through the midnight watches drear,
  And all the weary day,
O be Thy Good Physician near
  Our stricken one to stay;
That evermore as we succeed
  In service at his side,
Each office of our darling's need
  His heavenly hands may guide;

Till o'er his tempest bed of pain,
  His cry of perishing thrill
The Saviour's arm go forth again,
  The Saviour's "Peace! be still."

Too well, O Lord, too well we know
  How oft upon Thy way
Our feet have followed faint and slow,
  How often turned astray
For fleeting pleasures to forsake
  Thy path of heavenly prayer;
We have deserved that Thou shouldst take
  Our children from our care.
Yet, O Good Shepherd, lead us back,
  Our lamb upon Thy breast,
Safely along the narrow track,
  Across the dangerous crest;
Until our aching eyes rejoice
  At Salem's shining walls,
And to our thirsting souls a Voice
  Of Living Waters calls.

HE HAS COME BACK

Without the wintry sky is overcast,
  The floods descend, fierce hail and rushing rain,
Whilst ever and anon the angry blast
  Clutches the casement-pane.
Within our darling beats an angrier air
  With piteous outstretched arms and tossing head,
  Whilst we, bowed low beside his labouring bed,
Pour all our hearts in prayer.

Is this the end? The tired little hands
  Fall by his side, the wild eyes close at last,
Breathless he sinks, almost we hear his sands
  Of being ebbing past;
When, O miraculous! he wakes once more,
  Love glowing in his glance, the while there slips
  "Mother, dear Mother!" from his trembling lips,
"Dear Mother!" o'er and o'er.

He has come back, our little Fairy Child,
  Back from his wanderings in the dreadful dark,
Back o'er the furious surge of fever wild,
  The lost dove of our ark;
Back, slowly back o'er the dire flood's decrease
  The white wings flutter, only our God knows how,
  Bearing aloft the blessed olive bough
Of His compassionate peace.

SPRING'S SECRETS

As once I paused on poet wing
  In the green heart of a grove,
I met the Spirit of the Spring
  With her great eyes lit of love.

She took me gently by the hand
  And whispered in my wondering ear
Secrets none may understand,
  Till she make their meaning clear;

Why the primrose looks so pale,
  Why the rose is set with thorns;
Why the magic nightingale
  Through the darkness mourns and mourns;

How the angels, as they pass
  In their vesture pure and white
O'er the shadowy garden grass,
  Touch the lilies into light;

How their hidden hands upbear
  The fledgling throstle in the air,
And lift the lowly lark on high,
  And hold him singing in the sky;

What human hearts delight her most;
  The careless child with roses crowned,
The mourner, knowing that his lost
  Shall in the Eternal Spring be found.

THE LORD'S LEISURE

Tarry thou the leisure of the Lord!
  Ever the wise upon Him wait;
  Early they sorrow, suffer late,
Yet at the last have their reward.

Shall then the very King sublime
  Keep thee and me in constant thought,
  Out of the countless names of naught
Swept on the surging stream of time?

Ah, but the glorious sun on high,
  Searching the sea, fold on fold,
  Gladdens with coronals of gold
Each troubled billow heaving by.

Though he remove him for a space,
  Though gloom resume the sleeping sea,
  Yet of his beams her dreams shall be,
Yet shall his face renew her grace.

Then when sorrow is outpoured,
  Pain chokes the channels of thy blood,
  Think upon the sun and the flood,
Tarry thou the leisure of the Lord.

SPRING IS NOT DEAD

Snow on the earth, though March is wellnigh over;
    Ice on the flood;
Fingers of frost where late the hawthorn cover
    Burgeoned with bud.
Yet in the drift the patient primrose hiding,
Yet in the stream the glittering troutlet gliding,
Yet from the root the sap still upward springing,
Yet overhead one faithful skylark singing,
    "Spring is not dead!"

Brows fringed with snow, the furrowed brows of sorrow,
    Cheeks pale with care:
Pulses of pain that throb from night till morrow;
    Hearts of despair!
O, yet take comfort, still your joy approaches,
Dark is the hour that on the dawn encroaches,
April's own smile shall yet succeed your sighing,
April's own voice set every song-bird crying,
    "Spring is not dead!"

AIM NOT TOO HIGH

(To an Old English air)

Aim not too high at things beyond thy reach
Nor give the rein to reckless thought or speech.
Is it not better all thy life to bide
Lord of thyself than all the earth beside?

Then if high Fortune far from thee take wing,
Why shouldst thou envy Counsellor or King?
Purple or buckram--wherefore make ado
What coat may cover, so the heart be true?

But if at last thou gather wealth at will,
Thou best shalt succour those that need it still;
Since he who best doth poverty endure,
Should prove when rich heart's brother to the poor.

WILD WINE OF NATURE

IN PRAISE OF WATER-DRINKING

(After Duncan Ban McIntyre)

Wild Wine of Nature, honey tasted,

Ever streaming, never wasted,
From long and long and long ago
In limpid, cool, life-giving flow
Up-bubbling with its cordial bland
Even from the thirsty desert sand--
O draught to quench man's thirst upon
Far sweeter than the cinnamon!
Like babes upon their mother's breast,
To Earth our craving lips are pressed
For her free gift of matchless price,
Pure as it poured in Paradise.

BRIDAL INVOCATION

Jesu, from to-day
Guide us on our way,
So shall we, no moment wasting,
Follow Thee with holy hasting,
Led by Thy dear Hand
To the Blessed land.

Through despondence dread,
Still support our tread;
Though our heavy burdens bow us,
How to bear them bravely, show us!
Such adversity
Is but the path to Thee.

When our bosom's grief
Clamours for relief,
When we share another's sorrow,
May we Thy sweet patience borrow,
That to our Heavenly Father's Will
We may trust each issue still.

Thus our onward way,
Order day by day,
Though upon rough roads Thou set us,
Thy fond care shall ne'er forget us,
Till "underneath Death's darkening door;
We see the glimmering of Heaven's floor."

THE COMING OF SIR GALAHAD AND A VISION OF THE GRAIL

At the solemn Feast of Pentecost Arthur the King and his chosen Knights
Sat, as we sit, in the Court of Camelot side by side at The Table Round.
   None made music, none held converse, none knew hunger, none were
athirst,
Each possessed with the same strange longing, each fulfilled with one
   awful hope;
Each of us fearing even to whisper what he felt to his bosom friend,
Lest the spell should be snapped in sunder.

                         Thus we sat awaiting a sign!
When, on a sudden, out of the distance blared the bugle that hangs at
   the gate;

Loud the barbican leaped on its hinges; and the hollow porch and the
  vacant hall
And the roof of the long resounding corridor echoed the advent of unknown
  feet,
The feet of a stranger approaching the threshold step by step irresistibly:
Till opened yonder door and through it strode to this Table the Virgin
  Knight--
Strode and stood with uplifted vizor.

            Fear fell on all, save only the King!
  Uprose Arthur, unbarred his helmet; shone confessed the countenance
chaste.
  Then, for so the Spirit inspired him, set the youth on the Perilous Seat;
  Brake as he pressed it a Peal of thunder and paled the firelight, paled
    the lamps,
  Such a sudden stream of splendour flooded the Feast with miraculous light;
  Whilst, O Wonder! round the Table swathed in samite, dazzling bright,
  Passed the Presence, mystical, shadowy, ghostly gliding--the Holy Grail,
  Passed, though none could its shape discover, nay, not even the Virgin
    Knight,
  Passed, passed with strains seraphic, incense odours, rainbow hues--
  Passed, passed, and where it entered, suddenly melted out of sight.

ASK WHAT THOU WILT

Thy blood was spilt
  From death to set us free;
Ask what Thou wilt,
  'Tis consecrate to Thee!
Thy hands and feet
  For us the nails went through.
What is most meet,
  Bid ours for Thee to do.
     Ask what Thou wilt.

All round Thy Brows
  The Throne of Heavenly thought,
Divine Wisdom's house--
  For us the thorns were wrought;
Therefore, though dust
  In balance with Thy pains,
Take Thou, in trust,
  The travail of our brains!
     Ask what Thou wilt.

Thy Heart of Love
  With all its human aches,
By the spear's proof,
  Was broken for our sakes;
Our hearts, therefore,
  And all we love and own
Are ours no more,
  But Thine and Thine alone.
     Ask what Thou wilt.

Though homes be riven,
  At Thy supreme behest,
Yea! the sword driven
  Through many a mother's breast;
Thy blood was spilt
  From death to set us free;
Ask what Thou wilt
  'Tis consecrate to Thee.
      Ask what Thou wilt.

The Codes Of Hammurabi And Moses
W. W. Davies

QTY

The discovery of the Hammurabi Code is one of the greatest achievements of archaeology, and is of paramount interest, not only to the student of the Bible, but also to all those interested in ancient history...

Religion   **ISBN: *1-59462-338-4***   **Pages:132**
MSRP $12.95

The Theory of Moral Sentiments
Adam Smith

QTY

This work from 1749. contains original theories of conscience amd moral judgment and it is the foundation for systemof morals.

Philosophy ISBN: *1-59462-777-0*   **Pages:536**
MSRP $19.95

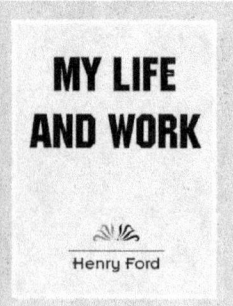

Jessica's First Prayer
Hesba Stretton

QTY

In a screened and secluded corner of one of the many railway-bridges which span the streets of London there could be seen a few years ago, from five o'clock every morning until half past eight, a tidily set-out coffee-stall, consisting of a trestle and board, upon which stood two large tin cans, with a small fire of charcoal burning under each so as to keep the coffee boiling during the early hours of the morning when the work-people were thronging into the city on their way to their daily toil...

Pages:84

Childrens   ISBN: *1-59462-373-2*   *MSRP $9.95*

My Life and Work
Henry Ford

QTY

Henry Ford revolutionized the world with his implementation of mass production for the Model T automobile. Gain valuable business insight into his life and work with his own auto-biography... "We have only started on our development of our country we have not as yet, with all our talk of wonderful progress, done more than scratch the surface. The progress has been wonderful enough but..."

Pages:300

Biographies/   ISBN: *1-59462-198-5*   *MSRP $21.95*

The Art of Cross-Examination
Francis Wellman

QTY

I presume it is the experience of every author, after his first book is published upon an important subject, to be almost overwhelmed with a wealth of ideas and illustrations which could readily have been included in his book, and which to his own mind, at least, seem to make a second edition inevitable. Such certainly was the case with me; and when the first edition had reached its sixth impression in five months, I rejoiced to learn that it seemed to my publishers that the book had met with a sufficiently favorable reception to justify a second and considerably enlarged edition. ..

Pages:412

Reference   ISBN: *1-59462-647-2*   *MSRP $19.95*

On the Duty of Civil Disobedience
Henry David Thoreau

QTY

Thoreau wrote his famous essay, On the Duty of Civil Disobedience, as a protest against an unjust but popular war and the immoral but popular institution of slave-owning. He did more than write—he declined to pay his taxes, and was hauled off to gaol in consequence. Who can say how much this refusal of his hastened the end of the war and of slavery ?

Law   ISBN: *1-59462-747-9*   **Pages:48**

MSRP $7.45

Dream Psychology Psychoanalysis for Beginners
Sigmund Freud

QTY

Sigmund Freud, born Sigismund Schlomo Freud (May 6, 1856 - September 23, 1939), was a Jewish-Austrian neurologist and psychiatrist who co-founded the psychoanalytic school of psychology. Freud is best known for his theories of the unconscious mind, especially involving the mechanism of repression; his redefinition of sexual desire as mobile and directed towards a wide variety of objects; and his therapeutic techniques, especially his understanding of transference in the therapeutic relationship and the presumed value of dreams as sources of insight into unconscious desires.

Pages:196

Psychology   ISBN: *1-59462-905-6*   *MSRP $15.45*

The Miracle of Right Thought
Orison Swett Marden

QTY

Believe with all of your heart that you will do what you were made to do. When the mind has once formed the habit of holding cheerful, happy, prosperous pictures, It will not be easy to form the opposite habit. It does not matter how improbable or how far away this realization may see, or how dark the prospects may be, if we visualize them as best we can, as vividly as possible, hold tenaciously to them and vigorously struggle to attain them, they will gradually become actualized, realized in the life. But a desire, a longing without endeavor, a yearning abandoned or held indifferently will vanish without realization.

Pages:360

Self Help   ISBN: *1-59462-644-8*   *MSRP $25.45*

QTY

The Rosicrucian Cosmo-Conception Mystic Christianity *by Max Heindel*　ISBN: *1-59462-188-8*　**$38.95**
The Rosicrucian Cosmo-conception is not dogmatic, neither does it appeal to any other authority than the reason of the student. It is: not controversial, but is: sent forth in the, hope that it may help to clear...　New Age/Religion Pages 646

Abandonment To Divine Providence *by Jean-Pierre de Caussade*　ISBN: *1-59462-228-0*　**$25.95**
"The Rev. Jean Pierre de Caussade was one of the most remarkable spiritual writers of the Society of Jesus in France in the 18th Century. His death took place at Toulouse in 1751. His works have gone through many editions and have been republished...　Inspirational/Religion Pages 400

Mental Chemistry *by Charles Haanel*　ISBN: *1-59462-192-6*　**$23.95**
Mental Chemistry allows the change of material conditions by combining and appropriately utilizing the power of the mind. Much like applied chemistry creates something new and unique out of careful combinations of chemicals the mastery of mental chemistry...　New Age Pages 354

The Letters of Robert Browning and Elizabeth Barret Barrett 1845-1846 vol II　ISBN: *1-59462-193-4*　**$35.95**
by Robert Browning and Elizabeth Barrett　Biographies Pages 596

Gleanings In Genesis (volume I) *by Arthur W. Pink*　ISBN: *1-59462-130-6*　**$27.45**
Appropriately has Genesis been termed "the seed plot of the Bible" for in it we have, in germ form, almost all of the great doctrines which are afterwards fully developed in the books of Scripture which follow...　Religion/Inspirational Pages 420

The Master Key *by L. W. de Laurence*　ISBN: *1-59462-001-6*　**$30.95**
In no branch of human knowledge has there been a more lively increase of the spirit of research during the past few years than in the study of Psychology, Concentration and Mental Discipline. The requests for authentic lessons in Thought Control, Mental Discipline and...　New Age/Business Pages 422

The Lesser Key Of Solomon Goetia *by L. W. de Laurence*　ISBN: *1-59462-092-X*　**$9.95**
This translation of the first book of the "Lernegton" which is now for the first time made accessible to students of Talismanic Magic was done, after careful collation and edition, from numerous Ancient Manuscripts in Hebrew, Latin, and French...　New Age/Occult Pages 92

Rubaiyat Of Omar Khayyam *by Edward Fitzgerald*　ISBN:*1-59462-332-5*　**$13.95**
Edward Fitzgerald, whom the world has already learned, in spite of his own efforts to remain within the shadow of anonymity, to look upon as one of the rarest poets of the century, was born at Bredfield, in Suffolk, on the 31st of March, 1809. He was the third son of John Purcell...　Music Pages 172

Ancient Law *by Henry Maine*　ISBN: *1-59462-128-4*　**$29.95**
The chief object of the following pages is to indicate some of the earliest ideas of mankind, as they are reflected in Ancient Law, and to point out the relation of those ideas to modern thought.　Religiom/History Pages 452

Far-Away Stories *by William J. Locke*　ISBN: *1-59462-129-2*　**$19.45**
"Good wine needs no bush, but a collection of mixed vintages does. And this book is just such a collection. Some of the stories I do not want to remain buried for ever in the museum files of dead magazine-numbers an author's not unpardonable vanity..."　Fiction Pages 272

Life of David Crockett *by David Crockett*　ISBN: *1-59462-250-7*　**$27.45**
"Colonel David Crockett was one of the most remarkable men of the times in which he lived. Born in humble life, but gifted with a strong will, an indomitable courage, and unremitting perseverance...　Biographies/New Age Pages 424

Lip-Reading *by Edward Nitchie*　ISBN: *1-59462-206-X*　**$25.95**
Edward B. Nitchie, founder of the New York School for the Hard of Hearing, now the Nitchie School of Lip-Reading, Inc, wrote "LIP-READING Principles and Practice". The development and perfecting of this meritorious work on lip-reading was an undertaking...　How-to Pages 400

A Handbook of Suggestive Therapeutics, Applied Hypnotism, Psychic Science　ISBN: *1-59462-214-0*　**$24.95**
by Henry Munro　Health/New Age/Health/Self-help Pages 376

A Doll's House: and Two Other Plays *by Henrik Ibsen*　ISBN: *1-59462-112-8*　**$19.95**
Henrik Ibsen created this classic when in revolutionary 1848 Rome. Introducing some striking concepts in playwriting for the realist genre, this play has been studied the world over.　Fiction/Classics/Plays 308

The Light of Asia *by sir Edwin Arnold*　ISBN: *1-59462-204-3*　**$13.95**
In this poetic masterpiece, Edwin Arnold describes the life and teachings of Buddha. The man who was to become known as Buddha to the world was born as Prince Gautama of India but he rejected the worldly riches and abandoned the reigns of power when...　Religion/History/Biographies Pages 170

The Complete Works of Guy de Maupassant *by Guy de Maupassant*　ISBN: *1-59462-157-8*　**$16.95**
"For days and days, nights and nights, I had dreamed of that first kiss which was to consecrate our engagement, and I knew not on what spot I should put my lips..."　Fiction/Classics Pages 240

The Art of Cross-Examination *by Francis L. Wellman*　ISBN: *1-59462-309-0*　**$26.95**
Written by a renowned trial lawyer, Wellman imparts his experience and uses case studies to explain how to use psychology to extract desired information through questioning.　How-to/Science/Reference Pages 408

Answered or Unanswered? *by Louisa Vaughan*　ISBN: *1-59462-248-5*　**$10.95**
Miracles of Faith in China　Religion Pages 112

The Edinburgh Lectures on Mental Science (1909) *by Thomas*　ISBN: *1-59462-008-3*　**$11.95**
This book contains the substance of a course of lectures recently given by the writer in the Queen Street Hall, Edinburgh. Its purpose is to indicate the Natural Principles governing the relation between Mental Action and Material Conditions...　New Age/Psychology Pages 148

Ayesha *by H. Rider Haggard*　ISBN: *1-59462-301-5*　**$24.95**
Verily and indeed it is the unexpected that happens! Probably if there was one person upon the earth from whom the Editor of this, and of a certain previous history, did not expect to hear again...　Classics Pages 380

Ayala's Angel *by Anthony Trollope*　ISBN: *1-59462-352-X*　**$29.95**
The two girls were both pretty, but Lucy who was twenty-one who supposed to be simple and comparatively unattractive, whereas Ayala was credited, as her Bombwhat romantic name might show, with poetic charm and a taste for romance. Ayala when her father died was nineteen...　Fiction Pages 484

The American Commonwealth *by James Bryce*　ISBN: *1-59462-286-8*　**$34.45**
An interpretation of American democratic political theory. It examines political mechanics and society from the perspective of Scotsman James Bryce　Politics Pages 572

Stories of the Pilgrims *by Margaret P. Pumphrey*　ISBN: *1-59462-116-0*　**$17.95**
This book explores pilgrims religious oppression in England as well as their escape to Holland and eventual crossing to America on the Mayflower, and their early days in New England...　History Pages 268

QTY

The Fasting Cure *by Sinclair Upton*   ISBN: *1-59462-222-1*   **$13.95**
*In the Cosmopolitan Magazine for May, 1910, and in the Contemporary Review (London) for April, 1910, I published an article dealing with my experi-
ences in fasting. I have written a great many magazine articles, but never one which attracted so much attention... New Age/Self Help/Health Pages 164*

Hebrew Astrology *by Sepharial*   ISBN: *1-59462-308-2*   **$13.45**
*In these days of advanced thinking it is a matter of common observation that we have left many of the old landmarks behind and that we are now pressing
forward to greater heights and to a wider horizon than that which represented the mind-content of our progenitors...   Astrology Pages 144*

Thought Vibration or The Law of Attraction in the Thought World   ISBN: *1-59462-127-6*   **$12.95**

by William Walker Atkinson   *Psychology/Religion Pages 144*

Optimism *by Helen Keller*   ISBN: *1-59462-108-X*   **$15.95**
*Helen Keller was blind, deaf, and mute since 19 months old, yet famously learned how to overcome these handicaps, communicate with the world, and
spread her lectures promoting optimism. An inspiring read for everyone...   Biographies/Inspirational Pages 84*

Sara Crewe *by Frances Burnett*   ISBN: *1-59462-360-0*   **$9.45**
*In the first place, Miss Minchin lived in London. Her home was a large, dull, tall one, in a large, dull square, where all the houses were alike, and all the
sparrows were alike, and where all the door-knockers made the same heavy sound...   Childrens/Classic Pages 88*

The Autobiography of Benjamin Franklin *by Benjamin Franklin*   ISBN: *1-59462-135-7*   **$24.95**
*The Autobiography of Benjamin Franklin has probably been more extensively read than any other American historical work, and no other book of its kind
has had such ups and downs of fortune. Franklin lived for many years in England, where he was agent...   Biographies/History Pages 332*

Name	
Email	
Telephone	
Address	
City, State ZIP	

☐ **Credit Card**   ☐ **Check / Money Order**

Credit Card Number	
Expiration Date	
Signature	

*Please Mail to: Book Jungle
PO Box 2226
Champaign, IL 61825
or Fax to: 630-214-0564*

ORDERING INFORMATION

web: *www.bookjungle.com*
email: *sales@bookjungle.com*
fax: *630-214-0564*
mail: *Book Jungle PO Box 2226 Champaign, IL 61825*
or PayPal *to sales@bookjungle.com*

Please contact us for bulk discounts

DIRECT-ORDER TERMS

**20% Discount if You Order
Two or More Books**
Free Domestic Shipping!
Accepted: Master Card, Visa,
Discover, American Express